Survival

RACHEL WATTS

For the Fighters

Prologue

Researcher v13 stretched the subject's skin with gloved hands, searching for a vein that wouldn't collapse under the syringe. She worked fast, expressionless behind the plastic face mask of the clean suit. She avoided the subject's eyes. The room was silent.

The researcher had entered the room alone, pushing a trolley of equipment and the small case that regulated the air pumped into her suit. The subject, F154, was already standing in position, at the foot of the bed, back to the door, hands by her sides. Early on they sometimes protested. Sometimes they fought. But F154 had been in the cell for long enough. She knew there was no way out. Only parts of her ever left the room, in her blood and tissue samples. If only she knew how full a life they would lead in test tubes and petri dishes all over the complex. The gift of her very construction, taken unwillingly, but a gift all the same.

v13 finished taking the samples, removed the tourniquet one-handed, and replaced the equipment on the trolley slowly and deliberately. Carelessness could be deadly. She gestured to the subject to climb onto the bed, as she powered up the ultrasound. The researcher did her customary mental arithmetic, the implantation date, time elapsed. She lifted F154's light blue hospital gown with a touch that couldn't be mistaken for tenderness. It was important to remain detached. With hard fingers she examined the subject's abdomen.

F154 stared blankly through the glass ceiling, at the vents and ducts above, linking the air in her cell to the filter at the end of the hall. The grainy image appeared on the ultrasound screen, pulling in and out of focus drunkenly as the sound waves shifted. The researcher studied it for a moment, eyes narrowed behind the plastic shield.

"Three point five centimetres," she muttered into her suit microphone. "No evidence of prosthesis rejection."

She paused. The subjects were not supposed to see the tiny thing that coiled inside. But this was the moment, the tiny hesitation, presented without a word. She hesitated just long enough for the subject to glance across. In her eyes a surge of loneliness surfaced to fill the space between them. Then, almost imperceptibly, F154 shook her head. A tiny movement, with lips pressed together tight and thin.

The researcher switched off the ultrasound. Sometimes they didn't want to see.

She wiped off the wand and put the plastic cover back over the ultrasound machine. The glass door slid open at a prompt from her handheld touchpad and she left the cell, the door whisking shut behind her in a hiss of gasses. At the back of the hall, V13 deposited the samples in the locked box, along with the digital recording of the ultrasound. She left her mark on the bottom right hand corner of the company paperwork. Only a handful of people could trace the mark back to her. Otherwise, the researchers who had contact with the subjects were protected by anonymity. She replaced the equipment and reset the security settings in the hall. As she walked its length to the main exit she felt the eyes and ears of every subject fixate on her movement. Identifying her by her breathing, her unique footfall. Her paperwork may not have linked her to them, but they knew her physicality. Sometimes, even when they didn't make eye contact, she could feel them staring at her, right into her. In her suit, behind the plastic mask, she felt exposed. As the door to the hall closed behind her she felt the weight of all those eyes lift. Peeling off the suit mask, she took a deep breath of the filtered air, pumped hundreds of metres down from the surface, and glanced at the guard with a smile she didn't feel.

"Lunchtime, yet?" she said. "I'm starved."

Chapter One

The office towers stood with their feet in water and crowns lost in the haze above. Ava had no desire to enter any of them. The boy rowed the boat with barely a ripple on the surface of the water that engulfed the old business district. Ava shielded her eyes from the sun as they approached and the buildings reared up above her. The odd unbroken window could be seen among shards and empty sockets on their faces.

The boy manoeuvred the boat alongside one gaping window and heaved himself into the building, gesturing for Ava to follow. He had instructed her to be silent but Ava wasn't a talker. As he dragged the dinghy into the building after them, the knuckles of his spine showed through his skin in precise definition. She shifted the bag over her shoulder.

The boat dealt with, she followed him into the depths of the building. The stairwell was only partially lit, snaked with electrical cables and data lines from solar voltaic panels on the roof. It was like creeping into the depths of a living organism. The doors they passed were identical and an armed guard stood outside each one, young all of them, teenage boys and girls, carrying weapons that looked heavier than they were. The building hummed with the mechanics of a small society. Hundreds of people living in close proximity, behind floor to ceiling tempered glass windows grown misty from their collective breath, several floors above the flooded city.

Ava's guide stopped outside one anonymous door and, with a nod to the boy guarding it, slipped inside with Ava on his heels.

"She's here," he said into the gloom and walked away without so much as looking at her. Ava was barely breathing.

Partially silhouetted in front of her were four people, two of them carrying weapons, the two in the centre with their arms crossed in front of their chests. The boy closest to her seemed young, too young to remember the world before, when the building they stood in was home to a business. People who spent all day working on tasks that would only need doing again tomorrow. Then they'd drive home to suburbs in vehicles, on streets that now lay metres under-water. Ava hadn't lived in this city before it was flooded but she knew what cities had been like; she grew up in Tokyo. The Tokyo of school days and skyscrapers, before it became a nuclear desert. To these young people, the world had always been half under water, the remaining landmass had always been a war-zone and living was just the space in between.

Ava held the backpack in front of her. Fruit, noodles and vegetables, in exchange for her sister.

"I brought what you asked for," she said.

One of the figures identified itself as a leader by stepping forward. She wore a shock of white-blonde hair and was older than the others. Perhaps she had once walked on city footpaths too.

"When you leave here you will forget about this place. Understand?"

Ava gave a stiff nod. One of the boys took her bag and slung it over a wiry shoulder.

"Sit down." The woman gestured to an old office chair. "And tell me how you know Sophia."

"She's my sister," Ava said. She returned the woman's blue gaze without flinching. You'll have no trouble from me, she tried to say with her eyes.

After a long moment she broke eye contact and her posture relaxed.

"We did some work for Sophia," the woman said. "Security tracking, mostly. She didn't need much help. She was very good at what she did, that's why the Boy Soldier recruited her. Until..."

"Until she didn't come back." Ava finished the sentence.

"We don't accompany people like Sophia out in the field," the woman said. "We just offer tech support."

"Look, I don't need to know what she was involved in. I just want to know where she's gone."

The woman looked up to meet her eyes again and for an instant Ava had a glimpse of loss. How many activists did she help? How many didn't come back? It was a brief moment, and then she looked away.

"I'm sorry," she said avoiding Ava's gaze. "There's nothing I can do."

"What do you mean?" Ava swallowed hard.

"We intercepted a message; apparently she was taken by Scylla Corporation heavies. She's gone."

"Are you trying to tell me that Sophia is...dead?"

The woman found the courage to meet Ava's eyes again and she held them, answering Ava's fears with a long, mournful look. Ava looked away first.

Later, as a boy rowed her back to the heavily populated areas of the city, Ava felt strangely grateful to that stranger. The woman might have opened the door to something dangerous but Sophia chose to walk through it herself. At least this woman who carried herself like a soldier had looked her in the eye and told her that Sophia was gone. She'd ended the long nights of waiting, yearning to hear Sophia's footstep on the stairs. She'd allowed Ava to think the unthinkable.

The squid leapt upriver, following the advancing tide, dark arrows above the water's surface. These were only a metre long, each obeying its own instinct to move upstream as the salt water encroached into the fresh. At least the bigger ones stayed in ocean, deep where it turned to black. Eventually, there would have to come a tipping point, numbers of predators that could not be supported by the food chain. But the changing salt levels and warming water had thrown everything that was known about ecology into the unknown. It was a new world, but to Ava it felt so old.

Ava gripped the railing of the ferry carrying her across the river to work and tried not to think. She had cultivated a reputation for being hard-nosed, tough, which served her well. Sometimes, when all she felt was loss, or fear, she let her dark looks and the tall-ships tattooed up her arms do the talking for her. Most of the time that was enough.

As the boat approached the far shore, grilled seafood and chili scents filled the air. Ava hadn't eaten properly in days and a rush of hunger left her reeling. Alongside it surged a memory of Sophia, pushing away the food on her plate and claiming not to be hungry. She would slip outside and offer the rest of her food to a kid on the street. If strength was Ava's protection, kindness was Sophia's. Generosity of spirit that neither the flood nor the grief could rob her of. And look how that had worked out.

She stepped off the ferry onto a punt sitting low in the water, nodding to the boatman as he wielded his pole. They didn't speak. Idle chitchat was dangerous. And anything could carry disease: a handshake, a coin, a kiss. At least coins and tokens could be boiled. Their value changed with the changing demands of the city. The air still carried the scent of burning human flesh from the pyres towed out to sea on barges during the last outbreak. Fear could draw people together and just as easily pull them apart. And there was something deeply disturbing about the fatty, almost edible smell of burning human. About the rumours of how the starving survived. The once unthinkable had a strange logic.

The water extended deep into the Southside suburbs but hawkers still sold their wares out of boats. Their shouts competed with each other and flies hovered thick around their piles of wares. The fishiness was layered with a deeper scent of sweet overripe fruit and rank vegetation. Ava gestured to the boatman to pull alongside a stall where she bought a bunch of bananas and calamari on a skewer. She chewed on the fried squid as the punter wove through stalls, eventually bobbing to a halt at a makeshift dock where the water ended. She dropped the coins she paid him straight into a jar of bleach he held towards her, and walked away.

Ava worked in Southern Oscillation, one of the few permanent bars on the Southside. As she made her way past the stalls that clogged the street, kids emerged from the crevices and shadows they called home.

"Hey Ava, whatcha doing?"

"You have any food Ava? A dollar?"

"What have I told you about hanging around here bothering the customers?" Ava asked them. The kids all shared the same grubbiness and wore a uniform of feigned indifference. They hunted in packs. Piranhas of the streets.

"Here." She gave the closest kid the bunch of bananas. "Take this and stay safe."

The kids scattered, vanishing into the small spaces that protected them.

The bar was on the second floor of an ancient weatherboard house, the walls shedding snowfalls of white paint as Ava's boots hit each timber step. Upstairs the room was drenched in murky half shadows, the day shift was ready to leave, and seated at the bar, a regular bowed his head over a house brewed beer.

"All right, then?" Ava asked, wiping the bar in front of him.

The man grumbled something into his beard.

"Just let me know if you need anything, mate."

Ava flicked on the outside lights and the bar seemed to grow, dominating the street with a winking leer. It was a friendly dive known for its abrasive staff just as much as for its cheap drinks. Soon, the place was packed and Ava managed the place with the deftness of a conductor.

"Ava, another beer?"

"Wait your turn, mate," she cautioned.

"Ava, how's about a smile?"

"Get in line, buddy," she quipped as she threw a wink at the colleague pulling a beer next to her.

As she served, she wore gloves and dropped the coins she took from customers straight into a bucket of vinegar and boiling water. Later she would fish out the coins and deposit them, still hot, into a locked box. She watched the bar with one eye, the street with the other and kept the bar open later than usual, despite it being quiet. In Ava's mind the silence at home, Sophia's empty bed, loomed. She needed distraction almost as much as she needed tips.

Later that night, Ava tossed on her single bed. In her dream, she heard the heavy boot of the security man's footfall on the stairs outside and sat bolt upright. She turned and saw Sophia, curled up in the bed across the room, the scent of fear and cigarette smoke clinging to her. As she watched Sophia slowly sat up bonelessly.

"Why did it have to be you, Soph?" Ava asked her dead eyes. "You have someone who loves you. Why couldn't someone else fight those battles?"

"You think everyone in the resistance isn't loved by someone?" Sophia's empty shell responded.

"You didn't have to take responsibility for this."

"But it is my responsibility. And it's yours. We live in it." Her voice was expressionless coming from a deep emptiness.

"I don't even know what you're fighting. Who you're fighting."

"Yes you do. You just choose not to face it." Sophia's head jerked forward on a limp neck. Ava couldn't remember the last time she'd seen her sister's easy smile. "Ignorance is cheap, Ava. Then it costs you everything." The light shifted and Ava saw Sophia's face was whittled down to the skull, her eyes sockets, her lipless mouth locked in a forever bony grin.

Chapter Two

The streets of the Complex were quiet by the time Valerie Newlin left the underground labs for home. It was getting dark and the transportables that housed the single residents were lit up from the inside. They'd be sitting down to a meal of food grown in Scylla Corporation gardens, from seeds developed in Corporation labs. Further away, her own brick and mortar house sat in a compact row of ten others, homes for families and senior staff. Corporation board members and high-profile staff lived in bunkers deep underground. Perhaps her mother had been offered a home there? Perhaps that might have saved her? The thought writhed acidic in her stomach. She wasn't sure if she was more afraid that the Corporation couldn't have saved her mother, or that it wouldn't have even tried.

The smell of noodles and vegetables hit her as she walked into her own front door. In wordless grief, her foster brother Lucas had stepped into the chasm left by her mother's death, preparing meals and keeping the house ticking. Valerie had discovered an inexplicable resentment as he took over tasks her mother had owned in life. True to form, he was in the kitchen as Valerie walked in, dishing out strands of stir-fry and noodles into two bowls. A third sat empty on the counter.

"No sign of life from your father?"

"He's buried in new test results." Valerie took her own bowl and sat down at the table. "I made him turn off the computer before I left, but that doesn't mean he won't find something else that needs doing."

"I think he's avoiding coming home," Lucas' voice was serious. "I know David's always been focused on his work, but don't you think he needs to spend time with his family right now?"

"We all cope differently."

"Mmmm."

They ate in silence. Outside, the alarm from the laboratory exhaust sounded in the humid night, an exchange of gases deep in the facility having breached some upper limit. The bell rang for the prescribed twenty seconds and stopped as the pressures within equalised. Valerie realised she'd been holding her breath.

"How are you, Val? How are you coping?" Lucas put a gentle hand on top of hers. She slipped her hand out from underneath his and cupped her bowl, relishing the warmth.

"I'm getting by."

Lucas looked like he was going to push the subject but his head turned at the sound of the front door opening.

"Don't panic," David called through the house. "I just thought I might come home before midnight and see my family for a change."

He accepted the bowl of food Lucas offered and sat at the table next to Valerie.

"Change is as good as a holiday they say, Dad," she said, shooting him a grin.

"Well, we're all due for one of those." David smiled back and started to eat.

"I learnt some new things today."

"Oh yeah? That lab tech's not giving you trouble, is he? He can be prickly."

"Nah, he's just shy."

"Got him wrapped around your little finger, I bet."

"I dunno, he seems nice enough."

"We're lucky you don't use your powers for evil, Val," David squeezed her shoulder briefly. "You could charm them into walking right off a cliff. Your mother was like that. She always saw the best in people too."

Her dad had sadness in his eyes, but warmth too, which was a relief from the emptiness that had taken up residence there. She gripped his hand hard.

She glanced over her shoulder to where Lucas stood, feeling awkward at being observed, and realised he'd already left the room.

Alone in her bedroom, Valerie took out the drive with the stolen files on it. She mouthed the word to herself, under her breath. Stolen. It sounded like an exhalation. Like a threat.

Scylla Corporation, the world's only surviving multinational, owned high tech labs and 12 floors of research facility deep underground. There it produced medicine, food from genetically modified seeds, answers to the new problems of survival facing the world. And in every city it had a lab, surrounded by a secure complex. A walled town for researchers, staff, their families and a huge security apparatus. In a world that had descended into chaos, Scylla was the law. And Valerie had stolen from it. She shouldn't still be within the Complex. Her heart raced, every cell in her body urged her to run. But nothing would attract suspicion faster. Act normal. Whatever that was.

A knock at her door gave her a start and, palming the drive, she turned to see Lucas looking sheepish in the doorway.

"What's up?"

"I just wanted to make sure you really are okay." He looked at the window, at the mirror behind her, anywhere but in her eyes.

"I'm fine Lucas."

"It's just, I lost my mother too. And my father." The Nguyens were a husband and wife scientist team, killed when the power station they worked at outside Tokyo melted down. Valerie couldn't remember Lucas ever having spoken about their deaths. Her curiosity was mingled with a little relief, because what could anyone say? How could anyone come to terms with the directive from Scylla Corporation to seal the power plant off, trapping employees and first responders inside.

Lucas met her eyes finally. "Grief can make you do strange things. Things even you don't understand. I know."

"I'm fine. Right now I'm just really tired," she said. Even when he reached out to her he was strange.

"OK. Goodnight then."

"Night."

Valerie stared at the back of the door Lucas had closed behind him, the first tendrils of panic growing inside her.

He was right. Grief could make you do strange things. She looked at the data drive in the palm of her hand. Things even you don't understand. She thought back, retraced her steps to the lab, around the computer terminals. Had she seen Lucas at all at work? Not for days. But still. He had looked at her so directly. And he had said, *I know*. Did he know?

She pictured Lucas' parents, entombed. Disintegrating. The device in her hand felt leaden. She wished she didn't have to carry it. But she knew no-one else would. She found herself childishly pining for her mother, to come in and allow her to spill her secrets and somehow make everything okay.

It seemed impossible that Mum could be gone. Her beaming smile, her loud voice. A short sickness, a sudden decline and death. Now the house—the whole world—felt empty. In the little data drive she carried a role she never asked for. And she wasn't even sure why.

It can make you do strange things.

Valerie took a deep breath and started packing a backpack, as the lab exhaust alarm sounded again in the dark.

Valerie left the Scylla Complex without a backward glance. Walking a block or two she peeled off her company jacket, leaving it on an overflowing dumpster. A few people loitering around pounced on the deposit. Let them have more luck with it, she thought.

She crossed the road and flagged down a motorcycle taxi.

"Head south," she muttered into the driver's ear as she climbed on the back.

The problem wasn't disappearing. The city was big and crowded enough that getting lost was always possible. The problem was what would come next. The northeast side was fairly orderly, with the Scylla Complex sitting above it, solar panels shining gold in the daylight. A beacon of wealth atop the sprawling, damp city. Further west and south, people lived closer together, their lives as fluid as the swollen river they lived on. Shanty towns or market stalls gathered in dry corners and disappeared just as quickly. Five years ago, at the height of the global financial crash, a dam had failed, flooding the low-lying areas of the city. People moved to higher ground, clustered on the sides of hills, wherever they could. It was like a new city but with less space to live, less room to grow, less food to go around. But even so, there was more to fish for in the flood water than could be found higher up the scarp. Large portions of the old residential and high rise business districts were all under water. Squid crews roamed every patch of water their boats could access, and children dropped a lure into water even the boats couldn't navigate. Such an overcrowded and mobile population made it easy for Valerie to get lost in the teeming city.

But what would she do with the data drive?

In the months since her mother's death, Valerie had become absorbed in her work. It was so orderly, so precise in the labs.

The totality of it, the fixation on things on such a small scale. She only wanted to see as much as would fit on a microscope slide. That was the size of the world she could accept without her mother in it.

But the stolen data. That was almost an accident. Almost. She had followed a research trail, absent-mindedly, with no thought of where it might lead. She was hypnotised by its unravelling, with a momentum all its own, spilling out blood types and assumptions. And then there it was. The truth. She couldn't put it back in the bottle. So she had made a copy and she had taken it.

Her mother had been so passionate. She was a woman of principle. Valerie butted heads with her almost weekly. And her father, a quiet man, demanded greater attention to detail. Analysis and critical thinking. In that moment, when she looked at the research data, things became clear in the way the fume hood removed contamination from the air. She saw the enormity of the wall between her peaceful existence and the suffering, sweating, starving city. The way those outside the Complex were considered totally foreign. Disposable. She saw that if she had stumbled across the secret, others must have known it too. And done nothing. And she couldn't accept it anymore.

Now, carrying a data drive with Corporation data, she was looking for answers. She needed to know about the rest of the world. Why the Nguyens were left to die. They were answers that her mother might have died for. She took a deep breath and was swallowed up by the city.

Chapter Three

Ava had barely slept. She sat in the punt trying not to look for Sophia's face among the faces that drifted by her. The gold solar panels of the Scylla Complex glinted from the scarp in the morning sun. She'd left home early, fleeing the quiet of her room. Her grief was so lonely. Her family was all gone, her sister the last memory of a time in which Ava was not alone. Now no-one remembered, there was no-one to share it with.

She was alone, but haunted. Every night her sister visited her in her dreams. In every dream, Ava begged her to come back, to turn back time and not get involved in the resistance, whatever that was. And in every dream Sophia told her she was already involved. That they all were.

"Ignorance is cheap, Ava," she repeated through dead lips. "And then it costs you everything."

Sophia became political after she met Dan. He had worked at the bar too, for a time, but he was what the older customers had described as "indiscreet"—prone to political outbursts that made everyone nervous, and eventually they let him go. But Sophia kept seeing him; she spent long days with him in wet suburbs on the Southside before arriving at work, mosquito-bitten and glowing.

Dan. The Boy Soldier. It had to be him. Whatever Sophia had become involved in, it was Dan who had led her there. He would have the answers. Perhaps then Ava would be able to let her sister rest. Perhaps she would be able to sleep.

The Southside suburb of The Bosch was permanently underwater. People lived in upper floor apartment buildings and stilt houses, the inconvenience of living below the tide level offset by affordability. And the ability to stay hidden. Bars, noodle huts, gangsters, poverty, everything that wouldn't sink floated down to The Bosch. Scylla barely existed; instead the area was ruled over by rival crime lords in an uneasy truce. Mosquitoes were dense and the risk of disease was real, but the crowding and the transience of residents made it a place to live off the grid. Surveillance cameras never worked in drowned suburbs. It was the best place to keep a secret. So long as you stayed alive.

Ava stepped out of the punt and walked through the floating suburb, feeling hundreds of invisible eyes on her. They settled on her, carved into her, made her brittle. She sat on a tiny plastic chair in one of the larger bars and ordered a beer. The bar owner was a slow-moving Islander, who eyed her warily. A small child ran around the edges of the platform, poking sticks into the fetid water. Insects droned. Sipping her beer, Ava tried her luck.

"I'm looking for a young bloke called Dan, do you know him?"

The bar owner looked at Ava with raised brows, as though she was surprised Ava could speak at all.

"Lots of people come in here," she said.

"This guy was political, young Indonesian fellow," Ava pushed.

The bar owner narrowed her eyes.

"He knew my sister. She's missing." Ava couldn't add the finality to Sophia's disappearance. She couldn't keep the desperation out of her voice.

"Lots of people come here. Some don't come back."

The bartender turned away and issued a whispered word to a boy Ava hadn't noticed, sitting at the edge of the platform. He glanced at Ava curiously, got up and ran away, bare feet nimbly navigating the rise and fall of the floating town. The air was heavy on Ava's skin, and she slapped at mosquitoes that may or may not have been imagined. Punts drifted past in a steady, near silent, stream. Hawkers didn't even shout from their stalls. The world felt slow. Waiting.

Ava had finished her beer and was about to move on when a man with a peeling face sat down at her little plastic table. He gestured for two beers over his shoulder without breaking Ava's eye contact. He was older than Ava might have expected at first glance, with thin orange hair and red skin that was pitted and broken, flaking off gently. When he lifted his beer to his mouth she noticed three missing fingers. He took a long draught before he spoke.

"I heard you've got questions."

Ava nodded.

"Not a good place to be asking questions, if I can be frank."

"I'm looking for someone who knew my sister Sophia. Japanese-looking woman, bit younger than me." It tumbled out in a rush, propelled by her racing heartbeat. "She's …" The words died in the back of Ava's throat.

"People go missing all the time. Sometimes they just don't want to be found."

"I need to know."

"It's safer if you don't."

Ignorance is cheap, Ava.

"Please. She's all I have."

He ran a hand over his damaged face, as though waking up, sighed and looked out over the water.

"What do you know?"

"Nothing. Sophia just didn't come home."

"Did you see the Wizards in the old business district?"

"Yes. They said she's...dead."

"So why are you here?"

"I can't... I don't understand."

"You don't understand death?"

"How could this happen to her?" Ava snapped. Her voice dried up as tears threatened. She held her breath, willing them away. She could not be weak in front of this man. As she fought to control herself, a ruddy hand with missing fingers dropped onto hers.

"Your sister was a fighter, love," he said in a low voice like honey. Ava could see how he might recruit a young person. Someone with nothing much else to lose. "Fighters get knocked down."

"Can I speak to Dan?"

The man shook his head. "Dan was shot. His body was given back to the sea."

Ava gaped at him. The tears finally fell.

"And Sophia?"

"No idea what happened to Sophia. Her body wasn't found." He leaned close to Ava. She could feel his breath on her damp skin. "But she's dead, do you hear? Or it's best you assume so."

Ava looked up. "Assume so?"

"There are things worse than death, love." His voice was a growl. "Either way, she's not coming back."

Chapter Four

Valerie woke on a rented fold out bed with one thought in mind: she had to release the data she had stolen. The thought came to her like an electric shock after a night of disrupted sleep and fluid dreams. She might not survive long on the run, and if worst came to worst she couldn't be the only person who knew what she knew. She needed access to the web. All night she had grappled with the precariousness of her position. The river had lapped at the bank outside, seeped through the cracks in her subconscious and pried open her fears. There were secrets buried here, it seemed to say, in the watery heart of the city. Her subconscious responded: *I know.* As morning dawned, she stepped out of the shack into a bustling marketplace, desperate to shine a light on it all.

When she had left the Complex, she had asked the motorcycle cab to stop at the first shanty town it drove past, somewhere for her to catch a few hours' sleep before moving on. She had felt she was out in the wide world, untouchable. But in the dawn she noticed the surveillance cameras on street corners. She was conscious of people's glances at her clean boots and her shining hair. She felt straight-jacketed in the humidity. She needed to keep moving. She needed to find a way to make the Corporation's data go viral.

She set off on foot and walked a circuitous route past docks and shanties, watching the other half—the people on the outside—living their lives. As the day drew on, a sour smell of river mud rose into the air and camp beds appeared in the shade of the stalls as it grew hot. The city felt viscous as the water and humidity shifted its shape. She took such an illogical route it took her most of the day to reach a ferry stand as far to the northwest as she dared. The jetty stood at an angle, victim of vandalism or high water, an impotent surveillance camera dangling from a concrete pillar. She leapt aboard the ferry at the last moment, reminding herself it was not a game she was playing. She remembered the pain her mother was in when she died. The Corporation hadn't even tried to save her.

She walked all day, toying with options. Eventually, she found herself underneath the sign at the front of Southern Oscillation, the one that that boasted cheap beer and fast internet. It was worth a shot. Valerie had never felt so friendless; the fear threatened to consume her. She climbed the ageing outdoor staircase and shared a grim nod with the heavy-set man at the door.

"Internet?" she said, peering past him into the dim interior. The man jutted his head in the direction of an ancient monitor at the corner of the bar.

"No streaming," he said.

She crept through the bar, each floorboard issuing a weak

protest under her feet. She felt eyes follow her from every corner and was relieved when she finally sat in front of the monitor and conversations resumed. Clinging to the mouse like a lifeline, she sat, head low, trying to disappear in the gloom.

"Drink, mate?" Valerie looked up to see a Japanese woman, wearing tattoos and a smirk.

"Just a beer."

The woman served her the drink, and accepted a few coins in a gloved hand.

"I'm Ava," she said. "If your connection drops out just give me a yell." She nodded around the leering clientele. "None of these bastards will help you."

Chuckles bubbled to the surface of the bar's chatter.

"I'm Valerie," she flashed her a sheepish smile. "I don't expect the data line is secure?"

The corner of Ava's painted lip curled up in response.

"You'll want to secure whatever's in the bag, if you want to keep it," she said quietly.

"Thanks for the advice."

Valerie toyed on the computer for a few moments, moving slowly, thinking and rethinking every move she made. Eventually, she felt the bartender's eyes on her. The other side of the bar was periodically cloaked in steam as the woman lifted boiled glasses out of a dented steel sink and set them aside. But through the fog she could feel the eyes, piercing, prying.

"Quiet here today, then?" she said, for want of something to say.

"Quiet everyday." Ava leaned against the bar with one pointy hip and crossed her arms. "People gotta work."

"Of course."

"Not you though."

Valerie realized now that conversation was a bad idea. "I work nights." She ploughed on with a bright smile she hoped was disarming.

"'Course you do." Ava leaned over the bar. "Not my business to pry, but you might want to get your story straight soon." She winked.

Valerie stared down at the keys in front of her. So much for playing it cool. She smiled up at the stranger. "It's that obvious?"

"Hey, no big deal, everyone who comes in here has a secret."

"Oh yeah?"

"Not everyone asks for a secure line. Mostly because there's no such thing."

"Oh."

"It's just that, not everyone's as cool as me, you know?" Ava tossed her hair a little and looked back for Valerie's response. Valerie just smiled and shrugged.

"Anyway," Ava continued. "You're best off staying quiet as much as you can. Never know who's listening."

"Right."

"If it rains again this place will be packed within the hour, squid crews hate the rain." Ava turned back to the bar as she spoke, pulled a beer for a man with skin weathered into the texture of upholstery.

"Right." Valerie looked back to the monitor.

"You have any idea what you're actually doing there?"

"Not really." She felt regret stealing over her. Like a warm bath, it made her muscles feel limp.

"Might not be smart to sit there too long, then." Ava pulled her gloves back on and reached over to take Valerie's empty glass.

The bar receded into itself as Ava turned off the outdoor lights. The bulk of the night trade had drained out of the street, people gone to whatever damp corner they called home. Eventually, Valerie spoke as Ava packed up the bar.

"You worked here long?"

"Few years."

"How did you get into it?"

"I started out in the wet suburbs out east, serving from noodle stalls, worked my way further west 'til I got here."

"Know how I can get to The Bosch from here?"

Ava's stomach lurched. Her own visit to the floating town still sat sour in the back of her throat. The humidity, the insects, the truth.

"You don't want to go to The Bosch, mate," she said trying to keep her voice steady.

"Don't presume to know what I wants."

Ava looked up at Valerie's sudden change of tone. The woman's sunshine had vanished and she had turned to steel.

"It's a tough place. Especially at night."

"You seemed to survive."

Ava was overcome by the lump in her throat. She turned away and poured Valerie a fresh beer, shaking her head.

"I'm sorry," Valerie said. "I didn't mean to presume..."

Moments of silence passed. Ava didn't know where to begin. She wasn't sure if she had been struck silent by fear or resentment. This woman, hope streaming from her pores, what did she know about surviving?

"My mother died," Valerie muttered.

Ava tipped her head towards her.

"She got sick. Cancer they said. But who knows?" She gulped her beer. "I think they killed her." Her voice was a whisper.

"Could have just been cancer."

"Could have been." Valerie shuffled the mouse around on the bar. "When your doctors and your employer are the same people... let's just say it's a bad time to have a conscience. And there doesn't seem to be anywhere that's safe. Not there, not here, not The Bosch."

Ava realised this stranger was right. She had been so isolated in her grief, the pangs of loss gripping at her like starving children, she had overlooked the fear on the faces around her. The bowed heads, the tightness in their shoulders. The undercurrent was toxic.

"We've all lost someone." Ava worked to get control. Her fists were clenched; she forced herself to be hyper-conscious of the semicircles her fingernails dug into her palms. "Doesn't mean we need to be careless."

"I don't know," Valerie said, casting a steely eye across the room. "I feel like care has been missing from the world for a long time."

"My sister spent time in The Bosch," Ava growled. "She disappeared. Because she *cared* too much."

She didn't know why she said it. It just fell out. Her temper skittered away from her as she stood motionless behind the bar, grinding her jaw.

Valerie reached across the bar as though she wanted to take one of Ava's clenched fists in a gentle hand. She stopped short of touching her and just patted the surface of the counter instead. "I'm sorry."

Ava swallowed hard and nodded. She didn't trust herself to speak.

"I think I know what they do to the ones they capture." Valerie's voice was low, her eye contact tentative. This conversation was dangerous. A tense moment stretched out in front of them.

Before either woman could speak, Benny, still filling the doorframe with his bulk, yelled across the bar.

"We're still serving, right?"

The phrase set a flurry of activity through the building. Ava slid a stack of boxes over a panel in the floor behind the bar. Patrons slid devices out of sight. Outside, the old staircase groaned under the weight of slow, tactical boots.

A customer made eye-contact and, having received a small nod from Ava, slipped into the kitchen and out the rattling scaffold fire-escape out the back. Just as the boots reached the top of the staircase, Ava realized Valerie had not moved.

"Good time to log off, mate," she muttered without making eye contact. "Go see Jim in the kitchen. He'll help you out."

Valerie looked up, wide eyed and took in the studied calm in Ava's posture.

"Sure."

The boots were at the top of the stair and the men attached to them threw long shadows spiked with rifles. Valerie was still sliding off her stool. Ava mentally willed the woman, with her questions and her naivety, away. But she moved so slow, heaving her backpack over the shoulder and turning back to Ava. The boots had paused and the men stopped to yell back down to the kids gathering in their wake. Scylla. Ava's mind was screaming, and Valerie had turned back to her, she had stopped to say something but then glanced at the fierce set of Ava's mouth and changed her mind. Walked away instead.

The Scylla heavies were in the doorway, exchanging words with Benny, and turning, turning, but Valerie had evaporated. The kitchen door swung slightly and was still.

Quiet settled over the bar's interior, casual hands smoothed hidden pockets, and conversations resumed with an idleness that could be carved. The Scylla man in the doorway looked slowly around. A creak from the floorboards marked each heavy step as he made his way into the room. The rest of the Scylla team fanned out along the edges while patrons pretended not to notice. Eventually, after standing in the centre of the room for a few moments, the leader spoke.

"We're looking for someone," he said to the room in general.

"We are authorised to reward anyone who can help us."

No-one spoke. The Scylla leader turned around to peer into each edge and crevice of the room, his boots making a small, slow circle.

"Young woman, blonde," he said. "She's a serious security risk."

His eyes alighted on the kitchen door, and he walked with slow, purposeful steps towards it and peered inside. He indicated for Jim to move out, into the bar.

"Anyone else in there?"

Jim stood in silence. The Scylla man glanced at the rest of his team, two of whom clattered through the kitchen door. A rattle of disturbed pans emanated before the pair re-emerged, one issuing a small shake of his head. Their leader brought the butt of his rifle down on the back of Jim's head and the boy crumpled to the floor.

"Refusal to assist the Corporation is a crime." He waited for a moment, eyes darting from person to person. No-one met his gaze. "My team is authorised to take all necessary action to protect public safety. All necessary action."

He looked around for a moment longer before giving a nod to his team. The soldiers began filing out of the ramshackle building.

He waited till they were outside, all eyes for any potential threat on the street, before he moved to leave.

"We know she's been here. We'll be watching."

Not a head moved to follow his slow, steady movement out of the door. He turned to fix Ava with a long, hard look, before slipping on a pair of sunglasses and walking downstairs. The bar remained motionless. Eventually, the sound of boots on fallen brickwork receded and Benny gave Ava a thumbs up.

"We're clear," she said in a voice that felt unnaturally loud.

The cook, Jim, had manhandled Valerie to the window and shoved her out, closing the shutters behind her. She didn't even have time to scream before she caught herself on a rusted scaffold platform. More hands grasped her and pulled her down, in between the stilts of the building, in the dark, mouldy space where the moisture had gathered. A rough hand was pressed against her mouth and shining eyes stared at her wide.

No-one breathed.

A voice leaked out from inside the bar, the words and sense lost, the tone menacing. Movement from inside came as vibrations and creaks travelling through the floorboards above her head.

An age passed.

In time a voice drifted down from the window above.

"Clear."

The hand unclamped itself from her face and the man she was pressed up against shifted.

"Do you mind?" he said.

"Sorry." The tension made her joints stiff and she cautiously untangled herself, and clung to the scaffolding. She watched the man clamber out from under the building, pull a stubby hand-rolled cigarette from a pocket and light it.

"Gotta tell you," he said as he exhaled the smoke. "You're smarter than you look."

Valerie stared back at him while flexing and opening her stiff fingers in and out of a fist.

"Was thinking you'd scream, and I'd have to...." He drew his thumb across his throat.

Before Valerie could respond, the window shutters opened from the inside and he climbed back into the kitchen. She hesitated a moment, looking down the street around the building and, for lack of better options, followed.

In the long moments that passed, Ava turned away, busied herself finding something cold for Jim's head. Valerie watched her silently. Eventually the cook waved Ava away and she stopped, took a deep breath and blew it out slowly.

"Thought you were green, not stupid," she said in a low voice.

Valerie didn't respond.

"A threat to public safety?" Ava barked. "You?"

"I'm sorry, I had no idea they'd find me here."

The adrenaline and fear coursing through Ava's veins turned into rage instantly.

"What did you think, they run the world, but they don't dare go into the slums?"

"I was stupid."

"Damned right you were."

"I'm sorry I put you and your people at risk."

Ava snorted.

"Perhaps we could help each other?"

Ava stalked the length of the bar, twice, grinding her teeth.

"Where I come from two strangers helping each other isn't the done thing."

"No offence, but that might not be a good thing."

Ava slumped onto a bar stool and put her head in her hands, exhausted. As the adrenaline dissipated her mind swam with a confused, fluid fear.

"What are you talking about?"

"I know where they take them, the people who disappear. That's why I ran."

Ava turned her head in her hands and peered out at Valerie.

"Perhaps I could help you find your sister?"

"Look, I don't know where you've been, but around here when people disappear they stay disappeared."

"You can't accept it though, can you?"

"Doesn't matter what I accept. It's a fact."

"Doesn't mean you have to stand for it."

Ava sat up straight and leaned her lanky upper body towards Valerie. She settled her firm grip around each of Valerie's shoulders.

"I very much want you to fuck off right now," she muttered.

"You can't hide from it."

"I'm not hiding. I've. Lost. Everything." Ava punctuated each word by digging her fingers and thumbs into Valerie's shoulders.

"Good." Valerie winced. "Now you can do anything."

Chapter Five

The early morning light crept through the slatted windows, negotiated the city's grime, shone on its poverty and stole into the store room at the back of the bar. Valerie woke feeling stiff and ancient after spending a night on a makeshift bed of sacks of rice. After much debate, it had been decided that letting her leave would be more incriminating than letting her stay, the assumption being Scylla informants would watch the place until the tide turned in the morning. The early morning sun moved across the sky and eventually there was movement at the bar's door and Ava walked in, closing the door behind her.

"Coffee?" She gestured for Valerie to follow her into the kitchen.

"Sure, thanks."

"So, what's your story?" Ava asked after a mouthful of coffee had started her conversation skills.

"Don't have much of a story," Valerie answered.

"Bullshit."

"If you say so."

Ava fixed her with a piercing look, one slim eyebrow lifted as though she could stab her with it.

Valerie responded with a grin and a half-shrug.

"It doesn't matter anyway, you can get rid of me today."

"How long do you think you can run for?" Ava asked.

"Who knows?"

Ava sighed and looked Valerie up and down. Gripped by self-consciousness Valerie crossed her arms in front of her chest. So what if her boots were clean, her body well fed? But she knew: she looked fresh faced and tense. A tourist, not a local. She looked every inch like a rich woman on the run.

"What are your plans?" Ava asked her, ignoring the question.

"Just need to get to The Bosch, then I'll stop troubling you."

"You're crazy. You know that?" Ava snorted. "The Bosch is a gangster town. You won't last five minutes."

"It's not really your concern though, is it?"

Ava slid the boxes across the floor behind the bar, revealing a panel in the floorboards. Valerie watched her lift the planks one at a time and put them carefully to one side.

"You're not seeing this," she muttered through clenched teeth.

"OK."

Eventually Ava reached into the dark space under the floor and retrieved a bulky canvas bag. Inside, dull gunmetal. A miniature armoury. She rummaged inside and pulled out two handguns and bullets.

"Keep this hidden," she said, handing a weapon to Valerie. "The Bosch is a dangerous place. Don't speak unless you have to. Don't ask dumb questions. Don't even look at anyone if you can help it."

Valerie accepted the weapon and nodded, eyes wide and staring.

"Wipe that dumb look off your face," Ava said. "You think we defend ourselves with harsh language?"

"I've never fired a gun."

"Nothing to it." Ava was already replacing the floorboards. "Just don't shoot your own foot off."

They left the bar down the scaffolding out the back while it was still early, stole through the vines that clung to it and picked their way around the edges of the suburb, along forgotten alleyways and through rubbish pits. Moisture gathered everywhere and peaty smells of decay drifted from the spaces between buildings, from the cracks in the earth. It was still morning, but the walk to the square at the corner was a hot one already. Ava and Valerie walked in silence.

Ava wasn't talkative; she didn't have many friends, and she generally wasn't interested in making new ones. But Sophia, once she had found someone, she would latch on and wouldn't let go. Somehow, she felt Valerie was the type to cling on, until long after it made sense. Against her will, Ava found herself finding more similarities between her sister and Valerie. The openness for one. Some part of her found it irritating and she was wary of being unable to distance herself from Valerie. But another part of her felt drawn to the woman's easy shrugs.

They made their way as far as they could, staying away from main thoroughfares, but eventually had to emerge to cross the flood waters. They waited for a ferry, sitting at tiny plastic stools under the shade of a tarpaulin, bowls of green papaya salad in front of them. Ava ate fast, demolishing the meal before a street kid could approach for a handout. Valerie jabbed her rough chopsticks into the bowl, selecting small pieces of food at a time, chewing carefully.

"So, where are you from?"

"Around." Valerie waved her hand vaguely.

Ava sighed.

"I was from the city originally," Valerie said. "My folks moved inland after the flood."

They shared a silence.

"You?" Valerie asked, finally finishing her meal.

"Family were refugees from Japan. Mum was from Lahaina though. We took land on a small island. It turned to salt."

"Criminal what happened in the Islands."

"At least we got out."

"Must have been hard."

Ava resisted the urge to hit her. Of course it had been hard. Around the island the sea rose almost visibly. Tides of gyre plastic lapped into what used to be farms, drifts of carcinogenic confetti. The stark fingers of dead trees, rising into deathly blue sky in what used to be an island paradise. Ava's youngest sister had died on the island. Then her father and mother on the boat that finally gave them passage across the Pacific. The ocean was a graveyard for generations.

The word "hard" didn't do it justice.

Valerie fidgeted and started zipping her bag's pockets, making ready to go.

"I can't sit around like this, gotta keep moving you know?"

"OK, let's head to the ferry stand." Ava started walking. "But I'm telling you, The Bosch is a dead end."

"You never know Ava, be optimistic. Maybe things will work out." Another grin.

"Yeah?" Ava muttered. "Has that ever happened for you?"

Valerie's grin evaporated.

At The Bosch, they found a communal floor of an old apartment building, just above the water level, which lapped against the balconies and defunct air-conditioners. Valerie staked out a corner to call her own. Around them, families gathered in groups, a space on the floor the only home they had. Camp stoves held bubbling broth or noodles, steam and the smell of food filled the air, mingling with sweat and something else, the scent of humanity at close quarters. Ava stood and watched, hands on hips, a single raised eyebrow posing the question she didn't need to say out loud. She deserved an explanation. But minutes passed in silence. Eventually she turned to leave.

"I live in the Complex," Valerie said to Ava's turned back. "My parents worked for Scylla. I got a job in the labs."

Something small and cold started to take wing in Ava's chest.

"If you work for Scylla, what are you doing here?"

"I took something."

"What?"

Valerie crumpled. Those effortless smiles, not so effortless.

"If you had a way to improve the world, to show people the truth, even if they didn't want to know about it, would you do it?"

"What do you mean?"

"I have something. Something I took from the Scylla labs. They'll be looking for it."

"Can you tell me what it is?"

"It'd be safer for you if I didn't."

How many times had Ava heard that lately?

"I have to get going. You'll be fine here I'm sure." She gestured sardonically at the crowded communal space, the cracked windows that looked out onto a flooded world.

"I appreciate your help, Ava. You didn't need to ferry me here like this."

"Yeah, shame I can't bribe Scylla thugs with appreciation."

"I'm grateful."

Ava shook her head. "Not grateful enough to tell me what kind of trouble I could be in though."

Valerie opened her mouth and closed it again silently. Eventually she spoke.

"Don't you wonder why the world is like this?"

Ava didn't know how to respond. All she wanted was for Sophia to be okay. She didn't want to be alone. But she hadn't kept Sophia safe. Sophia had wanted to fight and Sophia had been lost to it. *Ignorance is cheap, Ava.*

She looked at Valerie, her intense eyes, a fist gripping all her possessions tight in a canvas bag. The world seemed to bleed at the edges: Sophia and Valerie asking the same question, sharing the same quest to know, to fight. The battle that Ava had ignored. She had kept her head low and watched from the sidelines as the world had taken her entire family. In a wave of insight that felt like drowning, Ava realised that she had been a coward.

"You need a secure line. I might be able to help you," she said. "But not now, not today."

"I can't wait long, Ava." Valerie's voice was a taught whisper.

"Come back to the bar tonight, if you can. Late."

Valerie stood up and took Ava's wrist in a surprisingly firm grip. "It's dangerous. Are you sure?"

Ava closed her eyes and took a deep breath.

"I'll see you around," she said. And she walked away.

Chapter Six

It was another quiet night at the bar. Even the street kids had dispersed. Ava served the regulars and fishermen with caustic efficiency. The afternoon with Valerie had left her drained.

Late in the night, she served a man dressed sharper than her usual clientele. An impassive Vietnamese guy with clear eyes. But she felt a jolt of nervousness when she saw the Scylla insignia on his jacket. She sweated as she poured his beer.

Ava was still a teenager when she had her first run in with Scylla Corporation. She and Sophia had been in the city for several months. Penniless but safe in their anonymity. A few nights on the streets didn't hurt them. She spent some time working on a floating noodle shop, but work was unpredictable and the suburbs were risky. She worried for Sophia. She had to find more secure lodging and a stable job. It was during one of her exploratory forays to the Northside dry suburbs that she first encountered a Scylla security team. They were stalking bricks and mortar restaurants and bars in a well to do neighbourhood, the kind frequented by Scylla Complex residents. Scylla security teams left the poorer areas alone unless they were looking for something or someone specific. But in the richer areas they needed to ensure the privileged were safe, so they'd throw their weight around. There were eyes everywhere, unblinking.

She had walked into a bar and asked about work when she heard shouting on the street. Through the window she could see a woman in tears, while some men ripped her bag out of her hands. Before she had even thought about it, Ava had dashed outside and turned to challenge them. But they were not just the thugs she was used to on the Southside, tough guys who got their kicks and a few dollars from roughing up women and children. She realised too late that they all wore that logo. She backed away carefully, hoping they might be too intent on their target to consider her intrusion but slowly the two men rounded on her, their faces equal parts shocked and menacing. One of them handed the bag to the other and focussed his complete attention on Ava. Her stomach sank as he approached her, head cocked to the side, walking slowly as if trying to catch a small animal.

"Disturbing the peace, are we?" he said.

"I didn't realise you were officers, I'm sorry."

"You didn't realise we were officers?" he said in a mocking tone. "You think we look like bag snatchers, is that what you're saying?"

"No, I just, I was inside and I heard..." Ava nodded in the direction of the woman who was aghast at the new development.

"You heard what? Two officers going about their business?" he said, raising his voice. People had stopped to stare at the confrontation.

"No, I just..."

The Scylla man closed the distance between them, backing Ava up against the wall, his face just inches from hers.

"You're just interfering in the protection of the City, is what you're doing." He edged closer, pressing against Ava, putting his hand to her throat. She tensed, trying not to breathe.

"I think you could be of some use to the City though, strapping lass like you. I think we could find a place for you somewhere in the security quarters." He pressed his hips into hers and tightened his grip. Tears leaked from her eyes.

"What? You don't want to do your duty for the City, is that it?" he said leaning forward, putting his mouth to her ear. She felt stubble against her skin and his moist, warm breath. "They all say that at first," he whispered. "But you'll come around after the officers have had a ride." She could feel his sneer against her cheek.

Ava tried not to squirm in his grasp, tried to stay completely still. Time stretched out for a long moment as she felt hot breath on her ear. Across the road a motorcycle crashed headlong into a cyclist both of whom had turned to watch the drama. The Scylla man loosened his grip as he glanced over. Ava took her opportunity, delivering a knee to the groin, a fist to the man's throat and without checking if she had hit her mark, she fled. She ran blindly, tears streaming, bumping into people on the street, stumbling and collecting herself. Finally, when her lungs burned and her legs had turned to lead, she ducked down an alleyway, took a couple of random turns through side streets in different directions, and stopped. With her hands against a brick wall, she vomited acid onto the ground. She struggled to catch her breath as every cell in her body strained to hear the sounds of boots coming up behind her. But none came.

From that day, she had avoided the richer part of Northside. But now here was the Corporation, come all the way south, to sit at her bar and smile congenially around the room.

"All right?" she said.

The Scylla man shrugged and drank his beer. The customers were acutely aware of his presence. He didn't look like security. If anything, he looked like he worked in human resources.

"Just let me know if I can get you anything else," she said.

"Actually, you might be able to."

Ava instinctively braced herself.

"You wouldn't happen to have spent any time in the wet suburbs recently, would you?"

"I go through two to get to work every day," Ava said. "Any chance you could just say what you mean?"

"My name's Lucas and I think you know my sister Valerie." He punctuated the name with a direct look. "I want you to help me find her, she's in danger."

"Not sure who you're talking about, mate."

"Yes you are."

"Hundreds of people come through here every day, you can't expect me to remember everyone."

"I asked on the street."

"Who?"

"The man who saw her leave here, with the Japanese woman

with the tattoos," Lucas smirked. "You don't sound Japanese though."

"You don't look like the brother of a white woman."

"You have to bring her to me. She won't trust her emails but she doesn't know how much danger she's in. You need to tell her I know, and I can help her."

Had the security team not already come looking for her, Ava would never have trusted this man. But why would they send this nerdy looking guy after the big guns? Perhaps he was telling the truth? But there was no way she was going to tell him how to find Valerie. And she couldn't warn Valerie without leading him right to her. Scylla owned the data lines.

"When a person says she wants to disappear it's usually because she doesn't want any old guy who walks into a bar to find her," Ava said. "I met her, yes. I don't know where she is. And I don't want to."

Lucas rolled his eyes.

"Don't be ridiculous, she doesn't know where to go, you had to have helped her."

"Really?" Ava tilted her head back. "Perhaps her brother doesn't know her as well as he thinks he does?"

"Adopted brother," Lucas said with a smile. "My parents were in Tokyo when the meltdown happened."

That sparked Ava's interest.

"My parents were Japanese refugees," she said. "I'm sorry for your loss."

Lucas shrugged. "I barely remember them."

"Look, I don't know where Valerie is, I just gave her some directions." That was almost true. "Give me a way to contact you. If she gets in touch I'll let you know."

She was almost certain Lucas would follow her home. She would have been frightened if he'd looked like a Scylla heavy, but he didn't. He looked like he had half a brain.

Lucas scribbled an email address on a piece of paper.

"Don't use her name. Don't use your name," he said. "I use encryption but you never know with Scylla. They have spies spying on their spies."

Ava nodded, tucked the paper into the pocket of her denim shorts and went back to work. She watched Lucas out of one eye as he finished his beer, shot her a dark look, and walked away.

Valerie ordered noodles from a Malaysian woman on a passing boat. She peered at the hawker, at the boat shedding its skin of paint. The woman looked at her blankly, and glanced behind her. A voice piped up from the back and a teenaged girl leaned into view from the deck.

"Mum doesn't speak English," the girl said.

The daughter accepted Valerie's money straight into a jar of vinegar. As she did, Valerie noticed the girl's absent feet and the garish stumps showing at an ankle and shin. Valerie wondered at the infection that made such a crude amputation the best way to save the girl's life. At the amateur surgeon armed with dull blades and a saw. She glanced at the mother. She found she couldn't imagine the silent woman holding the girl down as the procedure was performed in a back room somewhere. But love drove people to desperate acts. Perhaps it was the only thing that ever would.

A multitude of fears circled Ava's mind. Like sharks they moved in and out of the shadows of her conscious thoughts, some coming into stark focus and then receding to reveal another equally valid one behind, crowding out rationality with muscular bodies. Lucas didn't know where Valerie was. Ava knew she was being used. But she replayed Lucas' calm expression, his shrug about his parents' death. It betrayed a certain kinship. A resilience to circumstance. She wanted to trust him. As she made her way home the tension generated by the humidity was as dense as the air. A steady flow of people surged alongside her, making their way to more promising fishing areas. Around the ever-changing, lapping water's edge the population shifted and swelled. The occasional fight broke out and was quashed. Ava paused to offer the women walking the streets a smile as she passed, which they didn't return. Every fresh gust of air, every slight change in wind direction filled hearts with hope that the rain would come tonight. Surely the weather would break soon.

She tripped over a bicycle left in front of the steps at the back of her house and swore under her breath. As she propped it up, she heard a sound from upstairs, something breaking, a crunch of broken glass underfoot. She shrank back against the building, under the shelter of a vine, hiding in its shadows.

She could hear the thump of boots on the stairs inside. Somewhere upstairs a woman was crying; the sound drifted out of the doorway on the humid air followed by heavy footsteps and two Scylla soldiers, tasers and guns holstered at their belts as they trampled through the garden.

"Set up a surveillance loop, send a camera station and guard," one of them said into a communicator. They walked around the house and their footsteps merged into the noise of the street.

Ava waited for a moment, barely breathing, before leaving her hiding place. She could hear her neighbour trying to stifle her tears upstairs. Finally, she emerged brushing off dust and leaves, and crept into the building, keeping her sneakered feet light on the steps she knew would creak.

Her neighbour was crouched in the far corner of her room, a hand pressed to her mouth to stifle her panicked sobs. The women made eye contact across the room, an exchange of fear.

"They've gone." Ava said, crossing the room to help the woman off the floor.

"They were looking for you, Ava."

"I know, it's OK." Ava drew a cup of water from the tank on the windowsill. "I'm sorry you had to deal with them though." She handed her the cup. The woman took it and shook her head.

"Don't be sorry," she whispered "Just be safe."

"You too."

Outside, a rumble of thunder made the panes of glass in the room's small window shudder.

She had no choice. Now, she too had to pack a bag and flee.

She would head back to the other side of the river and hope Valerie could meet her at the bar as planned. The dark expression on Lucas' face loomed in her mind as she crept back out of the building and into the street.

The rain, when it finally arrived, came in shotgun drops that sent people running to pull tarpaulins tight and close shutters. Ava made her way through back alleys as the flood waters rose. Old storm drains and service tunnels expelled their occupants: human, rat or decaying matter. All the things the city didn't want to know about floated to the surface as the rain settled in.

The streets were heaving. An influx of wet suburb residents, carrying all they owned, swarmed in between stalls, settling under the eaves of buildings. Ava joined the mass movement of people, head low, ducking watchful security eyes. At the river, the docks were filling with boats, mooring to wait out the rain. She climbed aboard one of the last ferries, succumbing to the crush of people, becoming part of the herd. She wore the desperation and sweat of the streets. She hid in it.

The ferries would only run for an hour or so after the rain started then the boats would be moored between city buildings. Ava looked at the faces around her, passengers who jostled and shoved, careless about what they never imagined they might lose. These people, their livelihood on their backs, would fare the best when the next long flood came. They would relocate to higher ground, indefinitely if need be, moving around as their fortunes changed. When the dam was breached in the throes of the crash there had been no resources to stem the flow down the scarp. Ava imagined the expensive riverside suburbs underneath the water beneath her. She had never seen them, but in her mind's eye they were pristine, open and friendly. Somehow she imagined Sophia in a place like that.

The street outside the bar was deserted by the time she got there, the bar closed up and dark. It's a shame the rain came too late to bring the squid crews in for a drink, she thought idly before remembering she had bigger worries than profit margins.

She let herself in and only had to wait fifteen minutes or so, with the rain coming down steadily outside, before hearing Valerie's light tap on the shutters on the kitchen window.

The women sat in the dark on the floor.

"Have you received any messages?"

"What?"

"I met some guy who said he was your brother."

"My brother?" Valerie looked surprised.

"Vietnamese guy. He wasn't armed. Didn't look like your usual security thug."

"Lucas." She looked pained. "What did he want?"

"He wanted you, Valerie."

"What is he playing at? Why would he be out here?"

"Well, to be fair I've had Scylla cronies in both my workplace and my home on the same day so I've got some bigger questions."

"This is exactly what I didn't want to happen," Valerie said. "I told you they'd be looking for me."

"You still haven't told me what the hell is going on," Ava said. "There were heavies in my house, they terrified my neighbour, and who knows who your brother is when he's at home. You say you know what happened to Sophia. I think you owe me an explanation."

Valerie stared intensely at the floorboards in front of her. After a time she drew a deep breath and started talking, without looking at Ava.

"I don't know for sure what happened to your sister. I told you I worked for the Scylla Corp. I was in the biosphere labs. They have whole teams looking at salt resistant plants, crops that could survive in tidal waterways, stuff like that. I was a junior researcher. I didn't deal with the big things. I didn't even know what half the research was for, I only saw small pieces of it, you know? Not the whole picture."

Valerie stood and started pacing.

"My father, he works in medical research. He asked me to help him with some data entry, no big deal. But I started seeing patterns. I started noticing cycles of experiment failures. Finally, I used my dad's ID card to take a look around the older records."

She sat down again and peered at Ava, her brow furrowed.

"Do you believe the ends justify the means?"

"It would depend what the ends and what the means were," Ava said.

"Right. Sure it would."

Ava looked at her confused.

"The experiment cycles that I saw weren't just failed experiments, they were human subjects," Valerie said. She stood with her back to Ava with her hands in the pockets of her cargo shorts.

"They're using people, and then killing them. Scylla is. Perhaps my dad himself. When they're done with them they're incinerated."

"I don't understand. How could they do that and keep it secret?"

"They don't. Plenty of people know. But they're the wrong people."

Valerie turned to face Ava, her easy-going demeanour gone. The fear was a tangible thing in her. Heavy and gelatinous. "Ava, something monstrous is happening. And I don't know what to do about it. I need your help. And I think it will lead us to Sophia."

I am responsible Ava. So are you. We live in it.

Ava jumped to her feet to shake it off, and paced a few steps back and forth before stopping to lean against the kitchen bench. Valerie stood behind her silently and put a hand on her shoulder.

"You said they were in your house?" Valerie whispered.

"Yes."

"It seems like you don't have much choice."

"I know."

"What will we do?"

"Your brother, Lucas." Ava turned to peer into Valerie's face. "Think he's on the level?"

"I honestly have no idea what he's doing out here."

"Would you trust him?"

Valerie looked around the room briefly and crossed her arms across her chest.

"I have no reason not to."

"We'll go then," Ava said. "We'll go meet him."

Chapter Seven

The streets were silent as Ava and Valerie emerged back into the square, people having found places to shelter while the rain filled every vacant crevice of the city. Ava led Valerie towards a corner of the marketplace where she knew boatmen plied their trade, ferrying people between drowned suburbs or renting out boats and letting them go it alone.

"Do you have any money?" Ava had nothing to trade but sex, and while she wasn't above that, it might not be enough for a boat.

To her relief Valerie gave a grim nod. "I have some."

The boatman charged more than Ava would ever have paid under normal circumstances but Valerie handed over a plastic bag of gold coins like it was nothing. The boatman's hand dipped as he took it from her, and his face softened, clearly relishing the weight of the coins, surely more than he'd ever seen in a single transaction.

"You ladies off somewhere important then?" he asked, eyes fixated on the money in his hand.

"For that price, we purchased your boat and your silence, mate." Ava growled. "You never saw us."

The man looked up and met her eyes again with a grin. "'Course not, never saw no-one. Not in this weather."

"Make sure you stay forgetful."

The man lifted a single hand in farewell as Ava manoeuvred the boat away from the dock in the rain. They sat in silence for a long time, Ava rowing the boat as the sky started to lighten in the east.

"Did Lucas tell you what he knows?" Valerie asked eventually.

"What do you mean, I thought you knew? Can't he help you?"

Valerie shot Ava a tense look.

"Why is he risking being out here during a flood, for what I know? Ava, how does he even *know* what I know?"

"But you grew up with him? He's unarmed. Is he intending to just talk us into delivering ourselves to the Complex?"

"I honestly don't know. This is uncharted territory."

"You know, the chances of us being taken back to the Complex at all are slim," Ava's breath was coming fast as she rowed.

"I know."

"Most likely thing is they'll kill us."

"Probably better than the alternative."

Ava stopped rowing abruptly and the boat coasted. "My sister faced that alternative."

Valerie took Ava's hand and gave it a squeeze.

"I'm sorry."

Silence.

The rain still fell solidly through the early morning light. Dense rain, the kind that could stay for a week. The boat they had bought was flat bottomed with a tarpaulin doing a passable job of keeping the rain off. In the deluge people gathered on the top floors of the apartment buildings around them. Debris floated to the surface or shifted just under the water threatening the boat's stability. At least, Ava guessed it was debris. She threw a pole towards Valerie.

"Use this to push the bigger pieces away," she said. "Keep an eye out for rooftops, they're low lying out here."

"Do people still live here?"

"Some do, in apartment blocks. There's a few who live on the water."

"Why would they do that?"

"Nowhere else to go."

An uncomfortable silence settled between them. Ava rowed through it with arms that felt weak. Disconnected from her body somehow. Fear was stalking her mind, trying to find a way in.

Eventually, on the southeast horizon a grey wall loomed, rising out of the water like the end of the world. Ava steered the boat towards the south side angling around metal shards and twisted gates. Finding an opening in the crumbling wall surface.

"What is this, a prison?" Valerie asked.

"A stadium. He'll meet us near the south entrance."

Tying the boat up to the gate, Ava put the oars inside and looked at Valerie.

"You think Sophia might be one of these test subjects, don't you?" she said.

Valerie looked around at the ruined stadium as though expecting it to offer her a solution.

"Or did you just say that to get my help?" Ava continued.

"I don't know. You said she disappeared. And I guess I needed someone on my side."

"I've been working so hard just to survive, Valerie."

"Is that what Sophia was doing? Just surviving?"

Ava's heart turned hard. "How dare you?"

"I just think that this involves everyone, including you. And I think you know that. You just won't admit it." Valerie leaned towards Ava in the rain. "I don't know what the right thing to do is. But I can't go back now. I can't pretend I don't know."

The sudden intensity on Valerie's face was like a cloud passing in front of the sun. "If you need to walk away and just forget all about this I'll understand." Valerie turned to clamber out of the boat onto the remaining grandstand. Ava watched her for a moment. What if Sophia was there? Imprisoned. Experimented on. Bare feet on cold concrete floor, syringes, serious faces of strangers hidden behind surgical masks. Even if she wasn't, could Ava live with herself if she walked away now?

"Can't resist huh?" Valerie shot back over her shoulder as Ava climbed out of the boat to follow her.

"I don't know why I'm doing this."

"Yeah. I know that feeling."

The stadium hugged a lake, its arching metal supports drawing the water into a rusty embrace. Water birds had made their homes through the grandstand and there were desperate clusters of plant life in the auditorium bowl. Somewhere underneath all that water were the remnants of a playing field. Lines marking things as simple as success and failure. Other than the white noise of the rain, the world was quiet. There was no shouting of hawkers, running feet of children; the air felt dense, wet but clean. Ava's nerves twisted as she followed Valerie, who was suddenly so sure of herself, to a waiting figure high up in the stands.

Lucas looked like he hadn't slept in days. It seemed so long ago, meeting him at the bar, the dash back to Ava's room, the Scylla team, the flood. Who knew where Lucas had been in that time? Glancing around, Ava couldn't see anyone else, but in the ruined blocks of chairs and support pillars there was no end of places to hide. She eyed Lucas' hands, still in his pockets, wondering if they gripped a weapon or communication device.

Valerie and Lucas simply looked at each other. Valerie seemed completely at ease in that infuriating way she had.

"What brings you out to a drowned suburb in the middle of a flood, Lucas?"

Lucas glanced around him. Ava followed his line of sight. There had to be someone else here. Scylla folks rarely went anywhere alone. Did Valerie know? She felt the hairs stand up on the back of her neck as she realised how very trapped they were. The rain held them all tight.

"What do you mean? Your dad's worried about you, he wants you to just come home." Lucas grabbed Valerie by the arm, her eyes widened. "Valerie, they don't know what you've done. But they will. Maybe they do by now."

"How do *you* know?" Valerie's eyes narrowed.

"You don't think your father couldn't follow your trail? You used his security clearance."

"But do you know what I found? Do you know about the experiments?"

Lucas dropped himself into a cracked plastic stadium chair. "I think I'd rather not know, to be honest."

"Typical," Valerie spat.

Lucas and Ava glanced at each other.

"I suppose you're just out here doing daddy's bidding," she continued. "Coming to fetch me back. That's always been your problem Lucas: no spine."

Ava interjected into the moment's silence that followed.

"What exactly was it that you took, Valerie?"

Valerie glanced at her in confusion, as though she'd forgotten who she was.

"I copied the data," she replied eventually. "On a portable drive. I have the proof."

"What did you intend to do with it?" Lucas' tone was incredulous.

Valerie turned her back to him, faced the bowl of the stadium, the water getting higher by the minute.

"I don't know," she said to the rain in general. "But I can't keep their secret now. I can't let them get away with it."

She turned to face Ava. "These people, Ava. They're subjected to constant surgeries that could easily kill them, having tests and samples taken. They're held prisoner."

Sophia rose up in Ava's memory, arguing about the politics of desperation: young, strong and so, so certain. Gone now. Perhaps that certainty was one of the secrets Scylla would have them keep.

Soon the piece of metalwork they had tied the boat to would be underwater. The ebb and flow of the river meant Ava was used to not staying in one place for long. But occasionally staying put was all there was left to do. She grabbed Valerie's arm more brusquely than necessary.

"We can't leave the boat there much longer. If you think we can trust him we should move it and get ready to camp here until the rain stops."

"I don't trust anyone right now," Valerie mumbled. "I don't even trust you."

The rain came down indifferently.

They made camp in near silence, each burdened by their thoughts. Eventually, having moved the boat, Lucas walked away with a fishing line and a squid lure, muttering about catching some dinner. Ava curled up and tried to sleep under the shelter of the grandstand.

Valerie walked the length of the stadium grinding her teeth. Seeds had taken hold in crevices at the water's edge and grasses had sprung up. Over years, decades perhaps, the vegetation would take the stadium back completely. Perhaps humanity too would be reabsorbed into the history of the planet.

The rain stopped as though someone had flicked a switch. There was a moment of uncanny silence as the earth adjusted to the absence. Then the world started to move. The air filled with the drone of insects and minutes later they were joined by birds taking to flight.

The water filling the stadium became still. Valerie speculated about the rumoured mammoth squid. She doubted they were in the city, clogged as it was with layers of humanity, from effluent of daily life to the vehicles still leaking oil on the ruined highways beneath the surface. But in the stillness, it was easy to imagine one giant creature, filling the bowl of the stadium, gazing up at her through a huge impassive eye. Valerie hugged herself, feeling exposed.

She found Lucas sitting at what used to be a window, legs hanging over the edge, jig line in the water. They sat in silence for a time, taking it in turns with the lure, imitating the rise and fall that was supposed to attract the squid just above the bottom. She couldn't help but picture the bottom outside the stadium, however many metres under floodwater it might be. A footpath probably, littered with broken glass, lost belongings that had sunk to the depths. She imagined the sea grass growing between the cracks where council workers once wrote parking tickets. Squid and prawns swimming where football fans once queued.

"What are you going to do?" she asked Lucas.

Lucas shook his head. "I'm not here to drag you back Val. It's like I said, your dad's worried is all. Perhaps we can help you?"

"I can't see how."

"What are you going to do?"

Valerie followed his gaze, fighting an urge to cry, to curl up and beg him to take her home. She had data she couldn't use. Even if she could release it, make it public somehow, would it change anything? Would people even care?

"People should know," she said. "This shouldn't come down to just me."

Lucas put his hand on Valerie's arm, and turned to her seriously.

"And it doesn't have to," he said. "But think about the risks you're taking. This is dangerous."

Valerie met his eyes and thought she saw doubt, or fear, in his expression. She wondered about the awkwardness that had always been between them, and wondered if Lucas could be a stronger ally than she gave him credit for. Perhaps even a friend. She had opened her mouth to say as much when Lucas gave a shout and started reeling in the line. At the end was a decent sized squid, looking as alien as ever, a prize for their patience. He hauled it over the ledge and killed it with surprising efficiency, wielding a knife Valerie didn't realise he had. Their moods lifted as they carried the meat back to the camp, pleased they had been able to provide for themselves.

After the meal of grilled squid, they collected rainwater into bottles and discussed the next step.

"You mentioned you could get safe access to the net?" Valerie asked Ava.

"Good luck with that, Scylla owns everything and scans more routinely than you'd think," Lucas muttered.

"I know someone," Ava said. She shuddered at the thought of going back to the old CBD, but it was the only option. The

Wizards would know what to do. "My sister was an activist. I know how to reach some of her old contacts."

Lucas' head snapped up at Ava's mention of her sister.

"She disappeared," Ava said. Her tone was a book snapping shut.

"Activist contacts?" Lucas asked.

"Sort of," replied Ava. "They're hackers."

Chapter Eight

They waited for the cover of darkness to cross the river. Still swollen from the rain, it would stay high for days, debris bobbing along towards the ocean. The mouth of the river, a delta of human waste, lost belongings, streaming out into the endless sea. Would it ever sink? Would it just float, meeting the gyres of plastic that still churned on the currents? Human civilization disintegrating but never quite disappearing.

The river went right into the old CBD, which was all but abandoned apart from the Wizards. Ava and the others sat in the boat silently, feeling eyes boring into them from the high rises around them. Most of the windows were dark but here and there a flickering light burned, shadows darted around them, grown huge and distorted by the strange angles. Ava kept her eyes fixed straight ahead as she rowed, explaining to Valerie and Lucas what they could expect.

"They're off the grid completely," she whispered. "Their net is filtered through so many proxies and red herrings it would take a bot a year to unravel it all. They support the resistance. For a fee."

Ava rowed the boat to the same ruined building the boy took her to last time she visited the Wizards, finding it again with only a little backtracking. They dragged it through a broken window together and turned, wet and cold, towards the stairwell. Ava's mind flicked back to all those guards, one outside every door, the whole way. She hoped someone remembered her from last time.

They were on the first landing when they were stopped. Boys with guns turned impassive faces towards them as Ava tried to explain why they were there. One of them whispered to another, who turned and walked away purposefully. After a few moments waiting he returned and he had brought another man with him.

"It's not okay to turn up without invitation," the man said. This guy was older, his sun-worn face creased beyond expression. "You'd better have a good reason."

"I'm Ava, was here last week."

"Cool story." The voice came out of the huddle of young men, the speaker hidden by darkness. Chuckles echoed around the stairwell.

"You lot, back to your posts." The older man spoke without breaking Ava's eye contact. The crowd dispersed

"I spoke to the woman with the blonde hair," Ava said, quieter. "I'd just like to speak her again. I have something new for her."

"Payment?"

"I have some coins and lots of Scylla credits," Valerie said. The man snorted.

"Not much call for Scylla credits around here, love," he said. "But I can take some of those coins off your hands."

"You'll tell the woman to see us?"

"No-one tells Dee what to do," he said. *Dee*, Ava thought. Just one practical syllable. "I'll make sure you get there safely though."

The door he knocked on was just as forbidding as any of the others. Dee herself opened the door, glanced with fierce eyes at the man who'd escorted them and made to close the door straight away.

"Wait!" His boot held the door open as he raised his open palms. "I come in peace."

"Go away, Mark," Dee growled.

"Some folks to see you is all," he said. "They don't belong here. I don't care one way or another, do what you want with them. But it's easier for me to not have bloodshed in my section."

Dee looked past him and locked eyes with Ava.

"You were supposed to forget this place," she said.

"Things have changed."

"Not my concern."

"Sophia could be alive."

The door swung open, and Dee stepped back to let them in.

"I'll deal with them," she said to Mark and closed the door on him. She rested her palms flat on the heavy firedoor after locking it, eyes closed, breathing deeply. When she eventually turned to face them she was as impassive as ever.

"Did you not hear what I told you last time?" she said. "She's not coming back."

"I need to know what happened to her."

Dee frowned and looked at Valerie and Lucas.

"Who are your friends?"

"She needs a secure line. She has data from the Complex," Ava said, gesturing at Valerie.

Dee raised her eyebrows and whistled softly under her breath, looking Valerie up and down.

"From the Complex? This sounds like a secure line that will cost you."

"I have money. Name your price," Valerie said, meeting the woman's eye with a direct look.

Dee held her gaze for a moment, as though sizing up the small blonde woman who'd barely spent a day in the sun. What risk was she worth? What danger would she put them all in? Eventually Dee just nodded briefly and turned to lead them into the shadowy depths of the building. The light was coming from diffuse bulbs scattered around the open office floor, cubicles once used for desks formed separate working and living spaces for who knew how many people. As she walked silently across the carpet on her combat boots, Dee greeted people who looked up. The wiring, power cables and phone lines, snaked along the floor, hung from the roof, meeting in spider web junctions at banks of monitors in various cubicles. At one end of the floor a tarpaulin flapped gently in the breeze coming in through a gaping floor to ceiling window. Elsewhere, cardboard had been placed against the glass in patches and further along the glass sat bare, reflecting the same cubicles and dingy light back towards them. Ava couldn't help but think of the darting shadows she'd seen from the boat down below and wondered how many people lived like this, secreted away, high above the water. Eventually Dee turned into one boxy room, and instructed them to sit at a small circle of office chairs before slipping away.

The three sat in silence. Around them the sounds of people living and working felt muffled against the carpeted floor. Overwhelmed by the space.

Dee returned with two boys, both dark haired and dark eyed. Brothers, perhaps, Ava thought, with a stab of loss as she recognised the shared mannerisms of siblings now that her own was lost. They introduced themselves as Tasker and Trang, and soon were engrossed in discussion with Valerie about the information and what she wanted to do with it.

"This is dangerous," Tasker said. "It's not your usual correspondence, we're taking a big risk."

"I realise that. I wouldn't ask you if there was any other way," Valerie replied. "I want to be the only person associated with this, they already know I've got it, you don't need to be implicated."

The brothers sank deep into a quiet conversation. Their hushed tones, and the way the space around them seemed to suck up every sound, crept into Ava's muscles as the sleeplessness of the past few nights caught up with her. Her head lolled and eventually, leaning against a carpeted partition, she slept.

The dawn was over when Ava stirred again; the light that came in the windows was white, the brilliance of the sun approaching midday, harshness dulled by the glass. The breeze coming through the absent window was warm. The days had turned dry after the storm. Gradually the humidity would build, making the world increasingly airless, until it became too much and there would be another inundation. The strange thing about the rain was the way it made it easier to breathe. For a time.

Ava was lying on a lumpy mattress, alone in a cubicle she didn't recognise. As she tried to gather her bearings she heard Valerie's laugh from close by, already familiar by its lightness. She crept out of the grey cubicle to find Valerie and Tasker, sitting by a camp stove with coffee cups in their hands.

"Morning Ava," Valerie said. "Don't panic, it's not quite the end of the world." She lifted the small pan off the stove, and swilled the contents gently. "There's still coffee." That grin.

Ava sat cross legged next to her and accepted a chipped cup gladly, the bitter hot coffee comforting her as she looked around.

"I fell asleep," she said.

Valerie nodded. "You were out to the world."

"Where's Lucas?"

"Off with Dee, getting some food."

When the others returned they ate, the six of them sitting in a circle around the little camp stove.

"Your cooking is appalling Trang," Valerie teased.

"Mate, I learnt on a boat," the young man responded. "The one you have to worry about is Tasker. If he offers you food, say no."

"This is why it never seems to be my turn to cook," Tasker grinned. "Only took one bout of food poisoning."

"Despicable." Valerie shook her head in mock outrage.

"What can I say? We do what we can in these uncertain times." The group dissolved into laughter.

It was as though they had all taken a deep breath, and the

tension they had been carrying evaporated. Ava found herself wondering how Sophia had got along with them, if she had shared the same jokes over vegetables and rice. Dee sat slightly to one side, smiling but saying little. She wore black clothes and combat boots, her white-blonde hair turning her into a photo negative.

It wasn't until the meal was finished that Lucas pulled out his communicator.

"Valerie." He was staring at the screen stony-faced. The mood of the group sank as Lucas handed the device to her with a shaking hand.

She sat looking at it for a while. Ava watched worry and fear pass across her expression, and her face grew serious, the molten metal that was her brightness solidified.

"We need to go back to Scylla," Valerie said quietly. They all stared. Dee opened her mouth and closed it again.

"They have my dad in custody." She put the device back into Lucas' still outstretched hand and wrapped her arms around herself. "I used his login, his security clearance. He shouldn't suffer for what I've done."

"But you'll be imprisoned," Dee said, finding her voice. "You could be killed."

"We could investigate from here," Tasker said. "Infiltrate their system."

Valerie just shook her head.

"Look, I know it sounds cowardly," Dee said. "But there's a reason we've all stayed alive for so long. Pretty much everything we do is illegal so we stay off the grid, even the solar panels on the roof were scavenged piece by piece. We make it work by laying low."

"They'll find us eventually anyway."

"That's what Sophia said," Dee replied. She was talking to Valerie but looking at Ava. "I told Sophia she was taking too much risk, there are better ways. Getting disappeared, or killed, it doesn't help anyone."

Valerie turned grabbed Ava by the shirt, pulling her to face her. Her touch was firm but kind, her face held fear and sadness, but also care. Ava wanted to walk away, go back to her little room, and forget the world. But she knew Valerie wouldn't let her. "Wouldn't you save Sophia if you could? Don't you want to know what happened to her?"

Held hostage by Valerie's probing eyes, Ava peered inside herself. Everything felt lost. If only she could know whether Sophia was alive. If only she knew if there was still something to fight for.

"My dad, Ava," Valerie continued. "I don't know what's happened to Sophia. But something awful is happening to my dad. It might not be too late for your sister, but if you stay here you'll never know."

Ignorance is cheap, Ava. Yes. She would do anything, even if it was just to know. She couldn't continue to be a coward.

"We should leave today," Ava said with a look at Dee. "The longer we're here the more likely they are to find this place."

Dee sighed and shook her head. But no-one tried to convince them otherwise.

The hackers gave Valerie access to everything they had, every proxy, every virus and every piece of intelligence. Then they removed all trace of her data from their system. When Ava, Valerie and Lucas left the tower of glass and steel it was as if they were never there. Ava watched the building grow smaller and blend into the other anonymous towers in the old city's centre as they rowed away, back across the river, back towards the Complex on the escarpment.

As Ava got off the ferry at Northside West, she knew the surveillance cameras were working just fine. She knew she was being sought by Scylla, she felt that same warm breath on her neck, tasted the bile in the back of her throat. She allowed herself to be propelled forward with Valerie and Lucas, and the closer they came to the Complex the firmer her fear took hold.

Valerie and Lucas on the other hand seemed more cheerful with each passing step. They were approaching familiar turf, after all. They seemed to speed up their pace and take even less caution as they passed through dry street after dry street. Once inside the Complex who knew what would happen, she had to be led by Valerie then. But in the blocks surrounding it, even looking too confident might catch the eye of a company man with something to prove. Ava told Valerie in urgent whispers to slow down, to avoid main roads, and stick to service alleyways and shadows. They needed to stay alive long enough to get inside. Eventually, just as they were about to cross a major thoroughfare she grabbed

Valerie by the wrist and pulled her back into the alleyway they'd stepped out of, Lucas following two paces behind.

"Ava, what's the deal?" Valerie was nearly shouting.

"Keep your voice down," Ava hissed. "They could shoot us on sight. They could keep us alive and torture us for as long as they like. You're an enemy of the state and you're walking along as if you own the place."

"But she *does* own the place, more than you ever will," a male voice snarled from close behind her. Very close.

Ava spun around and saw three pairs of Scylla security men.

"It's not often we take in a researcher's daughter," one of them said. He sounded impressed.

Ava turned back to Valerie, who backed away and crossed her arms.

"Ava, you know the stakes. One Scylla team or ten, we're looking at survival here."

Ava turned to see the Company men encroaching on her and when she looked back for Lucas he was already in the grip of a fourth team. She looked wildly at Valerie, hoping she had a plan. Valerie was speaking rapidly to a security man in a tone too low for Ava to hear. It didn't look like Valerie could talk her way out of a cell, Ava thought as she was forced to her knees by strong hands.

Chapter Nine

Valerie felt changed. Her mind burned with an anger she felt she'd had inside her for years, but only just recognised. The streets in the Complex seemed too clean and too quiet. Elsewhere, underground, labs would be buzzing with activity, gardens would be tended with waste returned to the soil as fertiliser. How much of that fertiliser was processed human remains? How much murder did the placid surface cover? As they approached the centre of the complex a neat row of rose bushes appeared, blooms the colour of blood, stark under the grey light. It was all too tidy, a charade as the world disintegrated on the doorstep. But also a nod and a wink to the initiated. We will always win, the Corporation said. People will drown, they will suffer, but it won't be us. Valerie felt ashamed.

The electric buggy they rode in, flanked by security men, turned a corner and started down a ramp. Valerie had assumed they would go straight to security processing but they had passed through that area. Now they were moving down into the underground labs. The most secure section of the complex. When they arrived at an unloading dock, security heavies marched a wide-eyed Ava down a concrete corridor, away. Valerie felt sick watching Ava's feet dragging, as the woman fought against the men's hands clamping her arms. She felt responsible for this brittle woman. *I will find you,* she made a silent promise. *Or I will find answers for you.*

Valerie and Lucas were shown through a different corridor, one that extended deeper into the heart of the science section. The security detail— two pairs, Valerie noted with satisfaction— left Valerie alone in a large meeting room. She wondered what punishment would be facing Lucas. Her fear-stricken mind leapt like musical scales through a list of potential crimes of which he might be accused, not lingering on any one note. It was easier to consider his fate, and Ava's, than to worry about her own. She waited without thought of what would happen to her, only idly wondering who might be coming to sit at the chair opposite her. Someone from security. They'd send people with just enough power to prescribe some kind of punishment, but no-one with any real authority. But Valerie needed to speak to someone in charge.

She waited and felt the surveillance camera in the corner of the room glare at her. She was as prepared as she thought she could be until he walked into the room—her interrogator. He sat down, laid a folder onto the table and opened it without a word. A few moments passed in silence. He turned pages with light fingers, engrossed, while Valerie stared at him, waiting for the calm to dissolve. David Newlin, her dad, sent to question her. It made a weird sense. He was a fastidious man. Precise, methodical. He had nursed his wife though her illness, he had grieved when she died. He had taken a short time away from the labs after her death before plunging back into work with even more vigour than before. David Newlin believed there was a right way to do everything, a steady application of scientific method, trial and error, careful documentation of results. He was not a man for conspiracy theories and he wasn't one to be bargained with, Valerie knew. She waited for him to start the conversation, to give her a hint as to how she could win back control.

"You have data from our secure medical system." He left the statement hanging over the table.

"Yes." Valerie said.

"I assume there's a reason for all of this." He phrased it as a statement not a question. "But I'm more interested in who you shared the data with."

"No-one."

"Why did you leave?"

"I needed to protect the information I had."

"But you haven't. It's back here after all." David placed the digital drive on the table in between them.

"I failed."

"I know you're not stupid, Valerie," David's voice was curt. "This is stupidity. Do you expect me to believe you stole classified scientific data, did nothing with it, risked your life in a flood, and then just came back?"

"I wanted to protect you. You shouldn't suffer for what I did."

David sighed.

"I was never at risk, Valerie," he said. Then under his breath, "You should have stayed away."

Survival

Valerie felt outside her body. As though watching from above, somewhere near the room's ceiling, she watched David pull one sheet out of the folder in front of him and turn it towards her, shifting it across the table with the fingertips of one spreadeagled hand.

"I want you to read this. It's the misconduct policy of the Complex," David circled his pen in the air above the last paragraph. "Someone else will be back to talk to you shortly." David stood, straightened his papers carefully and closed the file. "I recommend you be more helpful to them."

Valerie had expected shouting. Possibly violence. She wouldn't have been surprised if she was abandoned in a cell. But the calm questioning by her dad was not what she had prepared for. She watched David lift the chair he had been sitting in and place it neatly back under the table.

"Dad." She felt her face contort into a frown as though it belonged to someone else. As though her nerves had been frozen in ice.

He didn't turn back to her straight away. He stood facing the door, about to reach out to open it, about to walk away but also fixed to the spot, reluctant to take one step further into the future. He sighed and his head tilted downward, he stared at his shoes.

"Dad. What is happening?" Her voice was a whisper.

David Newlin turned back to face his daughter.

"Lucas," he muttered. "He gave you up, Val."

"What?"

David answered with just a raise of his eyebrows.

The blood stopped in her veins as she replayed his sheepish appearance at the stadium, his urging her to return, his sudden interest in the hackers in the old CBD. *I know*, he had said that night in her bedroom. That night she had palmed the thumb drive and waited for him to leave. He had planned it all along.

"I wish you hadn't done this Val," David sighed. His shoulders sank as he looked at her. He seemed older than ever. "Think carefully about what you say to them, will you? For me?"

Valerie swallowed hard and nodded. She watched as David pulled himself upright, turned, and left the room, closing the door behind him carefully so as to not make a sound.

She looked at the piece of paper her dad had given her. Residents could be imprisoned without charge for espionage, or for refusing to share information. Glancing at the document, she focused on the paragraph her dad had drawn her attention to. He had leaned closely over her while he had pointed at it, as though she were a child again, doing her homework at the kitchen table.

"Pay attention, Valerie," he would say. "The answer is right there in front of you."

Valerie looked blankly at the two paragraphs. They fell under a section describing the circumstances of an appeal.

"In the event of a threat to the security of the Complex, a resident may call for a trial. The trial will comprise a panel of his or her peers, and should be open to the public, with any eligible citizen of the Complex able to attend and give evidence."

There was a second clause:

"The nature of the threat, and its relative risk to the Complex, shall be assessed by the Complex Director before a trial be granted."

She would have to disclose the secret to the person who wanted it to remain a secret. Unless the Director had no idea of what went on in Medical. She had never met the Director, never even seen her. Valerie thought of people tied to beds, opened up to their very core, over and over again. Was that a technique the Director would endorse?

Ava woke in pain. She was on a metal trolley, in bitter white light. The blunt pain extended down her spine, into her hips, radiated down her legs. From where she lay, she saw only white walls, the hint of a door frame just at the edge of her field of vision, all bleached by the light from a surgical apparatus above her. She wondered if she had been drugged; she felt confused but oddly calm, as though she were standing a great distance away. She tried to wriggle her fingers and toes and got no response. The first feathery whisperings of panic stirred. She groped around her mind, for a memory that led to her being tied down or drugged and found nothing. The panic came again in a burst, loud as an alarm. Every cell in her body urged her to make a choice between flight or fight. She couldn't feel the tears that ran down her face. Her breathing came shallow and ragged.

The door opened with a click. Ava stopped breathing.

"Good afternoon, Ms Murasaki," a voice said, in a clipped accent. "I see you're awake."

***

When the door to the meeting room swung open again, it wasn't David Newlin who came through. Dressed in a security uniform, Lucas looked taller. More put together, somehow. No longer the bumbling junior staffer. He had a more direct way about him and when he sat down he chose the seat next to Valerie, rather than the one opposite. The folder and paperwork had gone; all he carried was a handheld screen.

"I said you still had time to go back," Lucas said in a disappointed tone.

"What the hell is wrong with you?" Anger coursed through her like a live current. "You said my Dad was imprisoned. The man who gave you a home."

"Yes. I'm sorry about that. It worked though," Lucas smiled.

"You're disgusting."

"I'm effective. Where did you have the hackers send the data?"

"You expect me to just tell you?"

"I'd like you to, but of course it's up to you." Lucas looked at her mildly. "We can be very convincing. Your hacker friends will discover as much in their own time."

"I know you Lucas, don't try to threaten me."

"I'm not threatening you. I'm not even trying to threaten you." Lucas leaned back in his chair and tilted his head, studying her. "It's of no consequence to me whether you choose to co-operate or not. My task is just to be convincing." He gave her a brisk smile.

Valerie had expected strong arm tactics. She had expected a tough guy with a penchant for crushing young women under his heel to come in, soften her up. Then maybe a department manager, maybe a director. She watched him slowly turn the screen on, flicking through files like it was another day at the office. Who was this guy? He was nothing like the shy, awkward Lucas she knew.

"Why are you questioning me?" Valerie said.

"Who did you email the data to?"

"Where is Ava?"

Lucas smiled again without looking at her.

"Where is she, Lucas?"

He met her eye and the smile dropped.

"She was remarkably difficult to convince," he said, as though he were talking about a confusing lab result.

He put the screen into Valerie's hands, on it a still from security footage showing Ava, in a medical gown, strapped to a trolley, unconscious. It was from one of the labs. Reaching over her, Lucas tapped a setting and the image changed, switching to a time lapse video of Ava, at first slow and drugged, then increasingly alert, then screaming. Her eyes were wide open, unseeing, tears streaming down her face. Her mouth was contorted mid scream, in pain, in panic. Her arms were strapped down but her fingers were splayed. Valerie couldn't look at her face, but as the time lapse continued to play, she watched those hands as they clamped down into fists, her body writhing. Finally, thankfully, the footage showed Ava asleep, an IV drip appeared and the video stopped.

"What the fuck have you been doing down in Medical, Lucas?" Valerie said, in a half whisper. But she already knew the answer.

Chapter Ten

It was a woman this time. Russell Smart didn't see as many women; there were fewer of them captured and when they were, they often went to the lab at the other end of the Scylla Complex. Women had valuable reproductive systems, they stayed useful for far longer. This one must have been faulty.

She sat in the steel chair on the other side of the glass, head lolling, still drowsy from the sedation. The Director of Research watched as members of his team, dressed in clean suits, face shields protecting their anonymity, strapped her to the metal. They started with her wrists, tying down the small hands that could lash out, grab, destroy. They bent down to restrain her ankles, one on either side of the chair, taking no chances. Lessons had been learnt since testing had started. The researchers were cautious. Finally, they stood either side of her and carefully passed the strap that would bind her head in place between their gloved hands, securing her skull against the back of the chair. The strap lay tight against her forehead, tangled brown hair pressed up against her skin. Her pulse beat evenly when the researchers attached the pads to the machine. The steady two-beat clockwork of animal life.

Having restrained her and hooked her vitals to the machine, the researchers left the room. They would come back with a trolley bearing a syringe on a stainless steel platter, a last meal the woman had not ordered. And they would administer the vital piece of equipment, the spinal connector, through which they would monitor the woman's deterioration. But for the moment he and the woman were alone, on opposite sides of the glass, her pulse the only sound between them. Russell surveyed her, surrounded by the rhythm of her heart. She was in her twenties. Possibly Indonesian. The memo had gone out across the city after a recent spree of violence against Scylla security. "The terrorists have been captured," a calm voice had told residents. Russell wondered if the residents would even notice. There was a limit to the human capacity for terror.

The researchers re-entered the room, bearing their gifts for the sacrifice. One stood behind her with the spinal connector; she seemed to look Russell in the eye before she slipped it into the socket surgically installed in the woman's spine. This was his invention. Russell imagined the solidity of the connection, the latch and hook that turned the woman's body into the piece of equipment they needed. He relaxed slightly as the information started to pour into the terminals in front of him. An analyst slipped past him and sat at the monitors, giving the researcher a thumbs up through the glass. Russell could tell it was Lucy behind that clean suit mask. The curt nod she returned could not be anyone else. Precise, methodical, the lingering distaste for her subjects that made her so good at her job. Russell had hand-picked his team, had chosen the people who would value the work they did, even as the rest of the world wouldn't understand it. Lucy was particularly adept.

The connection secure, the video cameras rolling, the researchers started the test. It was conducted wordlessly. The same test they had been doing for months. The woman, coming round from the sedative, was administered the cultured virus via syringe. The researchers' job done, they left the room. Russell knew they would be scrubbing down, removing the clean suits, out of sight on the other side of the specimen room. One of them would eventually present themselves at his side and he would be able to leave.

The woman on the other side of the glass was looking around her. Starting to panic. Russell heard the two-beat of her heart rise to a staccato, almost instantly. He smiled. Peerless design. But so vulnerable. He looked down at the monitors in front of him as Lucy walked into the little room.

"Ready to go," she said, expressionless.

"Timer's running," the analyst said.

"Call me when you see any change." Russell took one last glance at the subject and left the room. It could take hours, days, months, it seemed to differ from case to case. There was no point watching until the virus took hold.

Chapter Eleven

They dumped Ava on the floor in a tiny white room, and left her there, all limbs and pain, closing the door behind them. The linoleum floor was cool to her touch. She lay still, with her cheek against it, and focused on the sound of her own breathing. She used to do the same on the boat from the island. In the tiny, stinking cabin she would close her eyes, and focus on nothing but her breathing. Make it slower, make it even and calm. She practised being far away, on the ocean winds, through strong, steady breaths as the Pacific wrapped its arms around her. A calm ocean floor, with sharks drifting emotionless out of the black, circling, allowing her to admire their blankness, their cold eyes, their unwavering self-restraint.

She woke with a jolt, cold, and still on the floor. Propping herself up on her arms, the pain in her hips and down her spine came back to her. It shot through her as she moved. She breathed, steady and slow, and crawled onto a low narrow bed against a wall. There, drenched in cold sweat, she stared wide-eyed at the ceiling. She may have slept, for a time. When she next looked around she was calmer. She was able to focus her mind. The pain was a physical presence, a lithe animal sitting on the bed, staring at her, blinking slowly. She reached around her hips, to her lower back. Her pain lifted its head and flicked its tail, its cold eyes surveyed the way she was twisting. As she reached up her lower back, it sunk in its teeth. Pain tore through her flesh, but her head cleared as she felt something that wasn't part of her, lying nearly flush with her spine. Some little node of not-her, that didn't respond to her touch. Panic was back with her, and together with the pain, it nursed her to unconsciousness.

Valerie had seen similar tests done on mice. Watched the little creatures lie, unable to move, shrieking in pain. A spinal prosthesis. Turning the nervous system into a biological distillery. To apply the procedure to a person... her mind recoiled from the thought. But surely, that was what Lucas' images showed. Ava likely wouldn't move again. If she lived.

"Why?" Valerie whispered.

Instead of answering, Lucas allowed a slow smile to open his face. His eyes shone.

"What are you going to do with her?"

"That depends on you, to be honest." Lucas had turned away and opened a cupboard that Valerie hadn't noticed which was flush with the wall. As she watched, he pulled out a trolley, objects on top covered by a white cloth, and wheeled it alongside the table like a nightmarish tea lady. Valerie was confronted by a vivid mental image of a woman in a pencil skirt, hair pinned back in curls, pristine peach lipstick, serving tea to a table of men in suits. A world where tapping people's spinal fluid against their will was not a horror anyone had thought of.

She blinked and realised Lucas was looking at her, a question in his eyes.

"Whatever you want the answer's no," she said.

"That's a shame." He reached out and pulled the sheet off the trolley, revealing a series of stainless steel instruments, and gently fingered a narrow, sharp tool.

"This is the one we use to insert the prosthesis, on a patient like Ava," he said. He gazed at it, like a teacher might look at a child that was full of promise but proved to be lazy. He picked up a different, jagged device and held it up at eye height between their faces, turning it as though admiring the sheen on its serrated edge.

"This is what we'll use to take it out, when we've finished conducting our tests, should you continue to be obstinate." He smiled. "The choice, of course, is yours."

"Fuck you, Lucas," Valerie said.

A cold sweat covered her skin, her breathing was fast and shallow. Her hands clenched into fists, through no will of her own. Where would she run to, in this underground catacomb? Even the air was filtered before leaving the building. She looked back at Lucas who had busied himself with his trolley. Lucas had grown up as sullen as Valerie was optimistic. But he didn't seem withdrawn now. He admired the tools at his disposal calmly, straightening them. His shoulders were back and relaxed. Valerie had an urge to hit him. But the cameras were still watching.

She could still get a message out. She clenched her jaw and straightened her back to the table, ignoring Lucas. She spoke directly to them, whoever they were. The men in the shadows.

"Under the Extreme Duress section of the Complex Misconduct Policy I request a trial on the grounds that I have identified a threat to the Complex and to the continued survival of the larger city," she said clearly. "I demand to bring the evidence of what I have uncovered to the board of Directors in a public trial and that all residents of the Complex and the wider city bear witness and to test this evidence."

Lucas turned to her with a bewildered look. The meeting had gone off script.

"I demand that the city resident known as Ava be unharmed."

"What are you talking about?" Lucas growled. He was about to go on but he stopped, mouth open, to listen to a voice from the communicator bud in his ear.

"Out of your jurisdiction now, buddy," Valerie said, thinking of Ava, who could hardly help but finish a sentence with "love" or "mate". Valerie winced at the unbidden memory of her behind the bar, serving beers with the stoicism of an ancient sea dog captaining a boat on the Pacific.

Lucas stood without a word and rolled his torture trolley towards the door. As he opened it Valerie couldn't suppress a sneer at his deflated look.

"Did you think I thought you meant to torture me? You're not even wearing gloves."

Chapter Twelve

The room Valerie was shown into was a blank sheet of paper, but in the chips in the walls, the tarnished sink faucet, she read the stories of people who had been there before. It was a cell, really. Just wide enough to lie down in, just long enough to pace a few steps. Enough room for a narrow bed, and an institutional sink and toilet. There was a tiny table that folded out from the wall, and a chair. She sat on the bed, trying to read between the random scratches on the linoleum some clue as to what happened to those who came before her. Or some idea as to what to do next.

Hours passed slowly, the way they do when they have nowhere else to go. Valerie fidgeted, stared at the walls, and scratched itches that had long since vanished. When the door opened again, she knew it could mean more interrogation, perhaps even Lucas following through on his threats. The uncertainty almost insulated her from her fear. She was afraid on a visceral, animal level. The security man who walked in grabbed her by the arm wordlessly, removed her from the room and propelled her down a corridor. She felt herself thrust through another door, as though it were happening to someone else; she recounted the distance from the cell to this door, as though already telling the story of her escape.

The room she was pushed into was larger than the cell, with a couch and a separate bathroom. It was lived in too, with layers of crumpled sheets on the bed, stacks of paperwork on a small table. An odour of stale sweat lingered and something else, something metallic that made Valerie think of fear. A woman sat at the table, middle aged, and thin, with a bird's nest of dark hair, strands of grey showing through white. Her face was drawn; she looked like she hadn't slept in years. She wore plastic clogs, and lab scrubs that hung loose on her frame; her hands were gnarled and streaked through with the blue of the veins underneath. *Blood only looks blue through the skin.* The phrase came unbidden to Valerie's mind.

She examined Valerie with impassive eyes. Valerie wasn't sure what to say and when the woman didn't speak the silence seemed to fill the room, tightly packed cotton wool of unexpressed thoughts. She cleared her throat to break the oppression.

"They tell me you've asked for a trial?" the woman said. Her voice was raspy, as though unaccustomed to use.

Valerie frowned. "Yes."

"You're seriously seeking a public trial?"

"Yes. We should have that right, surely?"

The woman looked around the room as if searching for clues about Valerie from the walls, from the linoleum. Valerie wondered whether the woman's mind was still solid. She looked at Valerie suddenly, blinking as she made eye contact.

"You'll be waiting a long time."

"Maybe. My request was noted but it needs to be approved by the Director."

"It's hopeless," said the woman.

"Look, who *are* you?" Valerie responded.

The woman put her head in her hands and her shoulders started shaking. The convulsions became stronger as Valerie watched.

"Are you all right?" she said.

Finally, the woman turned around to face Valerie, tears streaming down her cheeks, mirthless laughter gripping her body. It took the woman like a seizure, coming from her very heart, out of her control. Gradually the spasm subsided, and she peered seriously into Valerie's eyes.

"It is hopeless, you stupid woman, because *I* am the Director."

The Director gestured to a chair for Valerie to sit in and turned away, eyes fixed on papers in front of her. She remained silent for so long Valerie wondered if she had forgotten her altogether. The woman somehow seemed aimless and focused at the same time; her wild hair and gaunt frame suggested mania behind intense eyes. As she read she scratched at her own arms, drawing red scores along her pale skin. If she was the leader of the Complex, this woman was not what Valerie might have expected.

Eventually the Director turned to her with a weary look.

"My name's Elizabeth," she said. "I've been the Director for 20 years, since before the flood." She stopped talking and her eyes wandered around the room, as though seeing her surroundings for the first time.

"This is the first time anyone has invoked a public trial," she continued eventually.

"Will you grant one?"

The Director leaned back in her chair and studied Valerie for a long thirty seconds. Eventually, she looked around her again, as though pointing out the cramped room, inviting Valerie to notice the squalid, dank smell.

"Does it look like I'm in a position to grant anything?"

Something tingled at the back of Valerie's mind, some memory trying to force its way to the surface.

"What do you mean?" But Valerie didn't really need an answer and the Director just returned her gaze. The room was not an office, it was not a place from which anyone ran a Corporation. It was a cell. The Director sat motionless for a time, letting the knowledge sink in, before leaning forward to pull up the cuff of her pant leg. Wrapped around her ankle was a tracking device.

"It measures everything, heart rate, location, I suspect it even tracks audio," she said. "I've been wearing it for 10 years."

Valerie swallowed hard. When she spoke her voice sounded smaller than she intended.

"Why?"

The Director gave a short smile. "Differences of opinion."

"With whom?"

"The rest of the Board," the Director shuffled the paperwork in front of her. "This isn't a dictatorship you know, there's a board of directors of which I'm the figurehead. After the flood, after things became so... challenging, we no longer saw eye to eye."

The tingling had formed itself into a memory, a vision of her mother coming home from work late at night, her face showing a weariness Valerie couldn't fathom. The Director wore that same look. The look of a fight that had gone on too long.

"Why are you still here? Why don't you leave? Or why don't they..." Valerie looked away.

"Why don't they get rid of me, you mean?" The Director smiled, almost kindly. "I'm not sure they'd want to." She paused and leaned back in her chair. "It's convenient for them to have someone else to give the orders, I suppose. They have no accountability. I'm recorded as having approved everything," she waved her hand vaguely. "All of this. But I've not been anywhere outside this room for years and years. Not without supervision by one of their guards, at least."

Her smile soured and she returned to the paperwork in front of her, lifting one sheet off the pile.

"Your mother was Sarah Newlin?" she said. "She and I got along well. I'm sorry for your loss."

Valerie fought hard against a lump in her throat.

"But it's only fair that I tell you," the Director continued, "The record will show that I was the one who approved her... treatment." There was a pause.

"What was she treated with?"

"Dimethylmercury." The Director's voice was expressionless. "She was dying months before she even knew she was sick."

"They keep records of that?" Valerie whispered.

"Every corporation keeps records, Valerie. You never know when they might come in handy. You just need to know where to dig."

Chapter Thirteen

It took four hours. Russell glanced at his watch as the subject started to writhe. She was exhausted. Not from the virus, it was too subtle for that. Her own panic had stripped her of the energy to do any more than lift her eyelids. But the disease inside her had its own desires.

He had to admire it. It was the ultimate stealth killer. He had already considered the resource wars, the strength of the virus to destroy an opposing force. Wars fought in the streets elsewhere in the world, where the Corporation had its forces heavily invested, protecting water, protecting fertile land. If only the subjects knew what greater cause they were part of.

Once the subject began to twist under the steam of the virus inside her, it was never long until the end. If she were on the street in the city, this would be the spasm that brought her down. She would lie on the footpath or in her bed, writhing uncontrollably. Her eyes were rolling back in her head, now strapped to the steel chair. The data in front of the analyst poured in. This was the gold at the end of the rainbow. The painstaking lab work, the hardware, the development of the spinal prosthesis. It had all led to these moments. This death rattle.

The woman's eyes were rolled back into her head, her mouth had started to foam as her body convulsed. Russell watched her hands open and clench of their own accord as the chair underneath her received the spasm impassively. Eventually, as the seizure took full control, her mouth opened and she gasped. The spray of blood and foam, of virus, antibodies, saliva and DNA, aerosoled into the air in the glass room. From there the convulsions grew distant, the storm had passed and now retreated. Her heart had a few uncertain beats left in it and then it stopped.

"Data is good," the analyst said into the silence.

"Quicker this time," Russell said to Lucy, who had appeared next to him.

"Yes," she replied. "We're getting good at this."

Out in the flooded city's CBD, Dee was working on some electricity connections when Trang ran up to her, breathless with excitement.

"Come on, it's time," he said.

"I'll be done in a minute," Dee said without looking at him.

"You'll miss it, come on!"

She left her work reluctantly, following the young man back to the terminals he shared with his brother. A group had gathered; word had got around. No-one was sure what would happen. Not even Tasker and Dee, who had helped Valerie with the upload, had filmed the message and had set the automatic delay, were certain what their actions would unravel.

"I hope this works," Tasker said as Dee took a seat beside him.

"It'll work," she replied

Dee had filmed the message herself, holding an old digital camera as Valerie calmly outlined information she couldn't believe. If it hadn't come out of Valerie's mouth she wouldn't have believed it at all. But Valerie had a certainty about her, a frank way of putting the data into words. And as she spoke, looking deep into the darkness of the camera in Dee's hands, Dee knew what she said was true. The surety sat across her shoulders, a new weight there, but familiar. Since the flood, since the crash, they'd always been living on borrowed time.

She and Tasker ran the message through as many proxies as they could, bounced it in every direction and ensured it couldn't be distorted or lost. It would go to the widest audience they could reach; it would spread like a toxin through the Corporation network and beyond, through the net and the phone lines operated by its wholly owned subsidiaries. Their minds swam with the scale of the work they were doing, the way they were writing the message large, across the southern sky and in the stars. They were turning the Corporation's control against it, for one precious, pre-programmed moment. It was as beautiful as it was terrifying.

She sat waiting nervously as Tasker reached over and gripped her hand.

"We'll probably need to leave here if this works," he said.

Dee smiled and glanced over at her friend.

"Wouldn't have it any other way."

Chapter Fourteen

Ava paced the white linoleum of her cell, walking five long steps from one blank wall to the other, between the two beds. She held her back straight and her spine taut, the only way she could avoid the pain that still ran through it, a dull ache, the animal slowly extending and retracting its claws. As she paced, Ava thought. She speculated, tossed around ideas, searching every last recess and forgotten corner of her mind for an escape route. Any reason for the thing that had been done to her. But ultimately, her mind circled around the locked door that stood in front of her, at one end of her pacing arc, solid and indifferent. The thing in her spine was too far out of her understanding. She didn't have a place in her world for it, it didn't fit. But a locked door? That, she understood. She paced, on and on.

She had been in the room for what felt like days. There were no windows. The lights went on at what she presumed was morning. They turned off at what she guessed was night. Twice a day a meal was passed through the hole in the door. Bread and coffee. Then thin vegetable soup. She drank from the faucet at the basin, and washed with a cloth in the same way. She could feel her joints stiffening and her muscles starting to become wispy. Sometimes she got uncontrollable shakes. Her eyes dried out and felt sandpapery. And always she felt the presence of the thing inside her. Settling into the groove through her spine, becoming part of her sinew. It seemed to stretch inside her, unmoving, unthinking. Her mind turned itself inside out trying to avoid thinking about it, the hideous reality of it. But it was real. Thin, but undeniable, like an electrical wire coiled through her centre. Humming as though it carried a live current. Unlike the flesh and bone it was coiled around, it was dead. Quite dead. But Ava was not.

She found her mind returning to Sophia, who might have spent time in a cell herself. She thought bitterly of Valerie. Wondered whether she was held in a cell next to her. Whether she thought this was all worth it.

Valerie slept in a light, tortured doze, her mind refusing to succumb to blankness. She dreamt she ran down endless corridors, and behind each door was another person she had let down, another person who would be tortured or killed. In front of her, at the end of the corridor, was the door that led to her mother. But it was so far away, and Valerie's feet couldn't carry her any further. She cried out but her voice wouldn't work, the words stayed trapped inside.

She woke with tears wet on her face, lying on the small couch in the Director's room. Across from her the Director sat in a chair, staring blankly at the wall. She had to wonder how many hours the woman had spent, simply waiting for something to happen. How could she have been a prisoner for ten years and no-one had known? How could she have signed the order for her mother's death?

As she roused herself she heard voices outside the door to the small room and she watched the Director's body tense. She imagined the door opening again and again over the years, with one more callous act demanded. One more lie. One more crime against humanity she had to perform. She felt cold rising up from her feet as the handle turned and the door swung inward. If the Director wasn't in charge of what went on at the Complex, who was?

The man who walked into the room was white and grey, a person copied from a printer running out of ink, and his thin grey beard hid a small mouth. His pale blue eyes betrayed fear, but also curiosity. He glanced at Valerie, before turning his full attention to the Director.

"The Board requests your presence,' he said.

"Nice of them to request. Usually I'm just ordered," the Director was muttering. Valerie couldn't tell if she were talking to the man or to herself.

"Let's go," the man responded. As he turned to leave the room he jabbed his chin toward Valerie. "You too."

They were led down the corridor outside, took a couple of quick turns and stepped into a large room, full of monitors, screens and people in varying degrees of panic. In the centre, 10 people argued around a boardroom table encased in a glass room. No sound emerged past the glass walls, and the fierceness of the argument was silently comical. Most of them were over 60, grey hair and slumped shoulders, shouting and waving devices around. They continued to argue as the grey man opened the door.

Watching the Director face the Board, Valerie noticed her height for the first time. The woman had none of the slouch her colleagues displayed. Though she looked tired, she didn't have the washed out look that the Board members shared. She was drawn up tall, her shoulders back, her eyes gleamed with fury. Valerie stood as far back as she could, her back to the glass wall, wishing she could disappear into it. She watched the Director's hands form fists, opening and closing once, twice, before the older woman walked slowly to stand at the head of the boardroom table.

"You summoned me?" she said in a loud, firm voice.

Mid-argument the Board of Directors looked around and, one by one, straightened their ties, smoothed their thinning hair, pulled out chairs and sat down. The Director alone remained standing, her palms flat on the table in front of her, leaning in and looking at each of the Board members in turn as though she chaired the meeting. Behind them the grey man quietly left the room, closing the door behind him.

"Let the record show that I, Elizabeth Wyatt, Chief Director of Scylla Complex South, highest authority in this State, have been detained under house arrest by the Board of Directors for 10 years, three months and 17 days," she said.

A woman seated at the table cleared her throat.

"There's no need for the same dramatics again, Elizabeth," she said.

"Regardless, I seek to have the record show that I am held as a prisoner."

"The record will show your statement, Elizabeth," a man spoke up from the table's far end. "But we have more important matters to consider. You are to make a public address."

The Director raised one eyebrow. "Am I indeed, Russell?"

"It has been written for you. You will be made more, ah, presentable first," he waved his hand towards the door. On the other side the grey man scurried into action, opening the door and moving to lead the Director through it.

"And if I refuse?" the Director said.

Russell raised his eyebrows with a half-smile.

"I think you know that isn't an option for you," he said. "But if you were to test our patience we would repay you by making things particularly difficult." His voice swelled as he warmed to his subject. "I think you'd agree that you have been living in relative comfort, for a good many years. We would see to it that that comfort would end."

"It hardly makes a difference," the Director muttered. The fight seemed to have left her. "Prison is prison, Russell."

Russell leaned forward in his chair and licked his lips.

"Oh, I think you'll find that isn't true at all," he said. And he smiled, showing a row of stunningly white teeth.

***

After the Director had left and the glass door was sealed, Valerie found the Board's attention turned upon her. Gone were the smiles. The sour scent of sweat and anger ebbed from the pores of each member of the board, pooled between the chairs and curled around her ankles. Valerie had no idea which monitors were networked, she couldn't know if the information had been leaked outside Scylla. But people deserved to know the truth, surely? Even if she remained detained? Or worse.

"It seems you've been busy," Russell said.

Valerie hadn't met Russell before, but he wore the lab coat and identity tag of a researcher. He could work in her department, somewhere on level 10, and she wouldn't have even known. He turned to a folder in front of him and read off a sheet of paper.

"Father, medical research. Mother, former public relations head, deceased." He glanced up at Valerie over the rims of his reading glasses. "Such a shame about your mother's sudden illness."

"Her poisoning, you mean."

Russell's eyebrows shot up. "Whatever could you mean by that?"

"You killed her." Valerie was almost snarling. "But I guess you didn't do it yourself. Had some low level flunky do it."

"That's a very serious allegation you're making." He was leaning forward again. Valerie didn't respond. Who knew what these people had done? Perhaps conversations like this were commonplace to them.

"Tell us who helped you," Russell said.

Valerie cocked her head. So the information was out. And the genie could not be put back in the bottle. Her fight to tell people what was going on in the Scylla labs was over.

"I released the results of medical trials on coerced subjects, with a deadly, and manufactured, virus," Valerie said.

"Yes. Who helped you?"

"I worked alone."

Russell's eyes narrowed.

"I embedded a trojan virus that installed a video on every Scylla networked monitor," Valerie continued. "Because Scylla owns so much of the network, I imagine it would have spread to most of the world."

"And then you returned here?"

"Yes. I didn't want my father to suffer for what I had done. When I was detained a timer released the emails automatically." Valerie shrugged and gave a half smile. "It was a backup plan."

Valerie sat in the glass boardroom as the Director appeared on the monitor on one wall. Through the glass she could see each screen in the incident room flicker and automatically display the same footage. The Director wore a grey suit jacket over a crisp white shirt. Her hair had been combed and pulled back, and her face was scrubbed clean and serious. She looked every inch the career politician.

Valerie realised she hadn't thought much further than getting the truth out. She had assumed the world would care as much as she did. As she watched, the Scylla Corporation wrapped the message up in a context as dreadful as the experimentation she had discovered. She wasn't sure if it was true or not. She wasn't sure which was worse.

"You may have heard that a release of unauthorised and untested information was made by a Scylla Corporation antagonist today," the Director was saying. "This release was unfortunate. It was also incomplete. I am Elizabeth Wyatt, Director in Chief of the Scylla Corporation, and I have important information to give you. I say this not to cause panic or concern, but to offer a full picture of the city's position now and into the future. I ask you to remain calm, and trust that the Corporation has put its very best staff onto ensuring the safety and wellbeing of every individual in the city."

A ticker ran along the bottom of the screen, describing it as an Emergency Broadcast from Scylla Corporation. Valerie wondered how far it would spread, how long it would take for her father, for Dee to be watching this very footage. They probably already were. The thought was oddly comforting. As though they were all crowded around the same radio, sharing the same meal, breathing the same warm air. She kept the image in her mind as the Director continued to read someone else's words off a teleprompter, electronic tracking device still strapped to her ankle, out of sight.

"The Corporation has detected evidence of a new, unique virus. It has spread through the populace and now threatens the health of every resident in the city. We do not know where it came from, or what causes it. Scylla researchers, within the labs in the secure complex, are working night and day to find answers. But what we do know is that this disease is deadly. And at this time, we have no cure or treatment. The city, it would seem, is dying."

Valerie's mouth was dry. As she watched she saw the slightest falter from the Director. Her lips pressed together tightly for a moment, a wave of uncertainty passed over her face. And then, the consummate professional, she kept reading.

"I realise this seems impossible. I realise many of you are not sick, and know no-one who is. But I'm afraid what I tell you is true. Carriers of the virus remain asymptomatic for many months, perhaps years. Further studies are vital, at any cost, to identifying the full extent of the risk."

The Director paused again. Her eyes fluttered from the teleprompter, to the camera, deep soulful eyes. Eyes of a woman you could trust.

"The Corporation does not take its responsibilities in this matter lightly. Its research, which some of you may have learnt of in an inaccurate and unauthorised release, is dedicated to facing this new danger. The research we do at our locations around the world including here at home is the only defence we have against this disease, which will destroy our way of life. We take this burden on, for our children, and for all of us. "

The flicker of doubt, of fear, passed over the Director's eyes again for a moment as they passed, in the most minute of movements, across some hidden teleprompter.

"Further, the release of faked research data indicates that the level of espionage, and the real risk of terror attacks in our city, is unprecedented. It is also the Corporation's responsibility to address this risk to safety and wellbeing of our citizens. A city-wide curfew has been issued and Corporation Peace Keepers have been deployed to ensure disturbers of the peace are arrested. As Director it is my solemn responsibility to maintain the ongoing peace and prosperity and I assure you, we will ensure those who threaten our way of life will be brought to justice." She took a breath as the tone of her address changed again.

"I wish you and your families safety, security and good health at this distressing time."

The Director blinked once, twice, three times before her image was replaced with the Scylla logo. Valerie felt instinctively, the way the hair on the back of your neck might tell you that a thunderstorm was approaching, that safety and security was out of reach for everyone in the city, tonight and every other night from now on.

She sat on the couch in the Director's room, numbed by the broadcast, imagining the panic that would, right now, be spreading through the city. In such an overcrowded, desperate city, panic was a wild beast. People would die. It was inevitable. Perhaps they already had. She had wanted to stir people into action. But this was too far beyond the idea of resistance. This would just spark fear. And in times of fear people would keep the Corporation close. They needed to know someone could do something. Valerie had never felt such futility.

Russell marched into the room followed by an ashen Director. He stood, hands on his hips while the Director climbed into her narrow bed and lay there without a word.

"It's true you know," he said. "You call us criminals, but we're all fighting the same thing."

The women languished in their private silences.

"Drink?" Russell said. Behind him a security man pushed a trolley carrying glasses and a bottle of gin. This wasn't the homebrew Valerie's dad drank. It had a label. It had to be an antique.

"We have to keep control," he said as he poured. "It might be an imperfect system, but the alternative is anarchy. It's chaos. Most of the city wouldn't survive."

"I think the city should have the choice, to be honest," Valerie said.

"You know, two hundred years ago the dam wasn't even built yet," the Director said from where she lay in the narrow cot. Her voice made her sound a hundred years old. "It was built when my grandparents were children. Before then this whole area from the scarp to the ocean was a flood plain."

Russell handed Valerie a glass. Real ice cubes clinked in it, floating to the surface. Valerie hadn't seen ice for years. She stared, almost unwilling to take a sip, hesitant to disturb the vision of something so cold and pure. So fleeting.

"Now a lot of it is flooded again," the Director continued. "It's back the way it was. We, all of us, can only hold back the tide for so long. Nature is inexhaustible, it is patient. It will take us all back too, eventually." She sat up abruptly and looked at Russell, menace emanating from her eyes. "You don't think you're going to live forever, do you?"

"No."

"The only thing we can do, right now, is buy time."

"But this isn't nature, is it?" Valerie said. "What they're doing in the lab. The flood. The climate. It's all human intervention. The best thing we can do is to let people decide for themselves. The best thing we can do is treat everyone fairly."

"People are stupid, Valerie. People are afraid and violent and self-serving. People as a whole cannot know what is right," Russell said.

"And the Corporation can?"

The Director sighed, her shoulders slumped. "None of us know. We're lost."

"Speak for yourself, Elizabeth," Russell said.

They sat in silence for a few minutes before the Director turned to look Valerie in the eye. "Have you ever seen a cat cornered? It will never back down, it will hiss and spit and try to look bigger. People are like that, sometimes the best defence is an offence."

"Are you trying to excuse this testing? This toying with the truth? Because that's what that message did. You took the truth and you put it in a cage of fear."

"Times are desperate."

Russell looked between the two women mildly, assessing them as if they were each a piece of art he didn't quite understand.

"Valerie," he said eventually, putting his glass down. "You still need to face punishment for your crimes."

Valerie's stomach sank.

"You'll grant a trial?"

The Director smiled sadly.

"Did you really think that was going to happen?"

Chapter Fifteen

They were political agitators, rabble rousers and conscientious objectors. Some of them were just in the wrong place at the right time. Antagonists to the Corporation, disturbers of the peace, the poor and the desperate. They lived together in a white hall, each in their own room with glass walls. They were fed intravenously. Their feet were bare. Their heads were shaved.

They were in the best physical health of their lives. They were healthier than the researchers who entered their glass rooms in clean suits, to take samples from their muscles, spines, brains. But their eyes were dark. They were being stolen, diminished, one cell sample at a time. They experienced no human contact. They were referred to by number. Even their names were taken.

F154 used to be called Sophia. She lived in the city, not far from the Complex. She was mixed up in a dangerous crowd. She became political. She believed the Corporation was an oppressing force. Her boyfriend, Dan, believed in active resistance. He was known as The Boy Soldier, though he wasn't a boy, not anymore. He had been developing contacts, amassing a fighting force, for most of his short life. He started in weapons: making, rebuilding and supplying arms to local thugs. He nurtured contacts in the criminal underground. Eventually, he had his own small team and the means to fight back. He wasn't sure where it would all lead in the long term and as it turned out the choice was made for him: shot resisting arrest, his flesh a home for a Corporation bullet. He got off lightly. There was no judicial system for political crime. For F154 there was just four walls of glass and a catheter strapped to her thigh.

She watched the people in the other glass rooms around her. She watched as they broke down, stopped responding. Sometimes, one of them would act out. Sometimes they would prowl their glass room, scream, rail against the glass walls. It wouldn't achieve anything. She had seen a security man fire a gun at the glass once. The subject inside ducked and screamed, but the bullet bounced off harmlessly, the reinforced glass shuddered slightly and then was still. The security man walked away, laughing, tapping his gun on the glass walls of the cells he passed. His target cowered in the corner, screaming, moaning and finally sobbing quietly. F154 was glad when he stopped.

She focussed on the heart monitor in her room. She watched its beat, methodical and slow, the line that represented her blood flowing through her veins moving forward, from her past to some un-nameable future. When someone became agitated, or when a security man came into the hall, it started to race. She could see the line leaping around and she felt her blood cells reciprocating inside her. She clutched at her chest, willing her blood to behave. It should be a dance, she would croon, under her breath, it should be a waltz.

She was humming a tune she'd never heard before when the door to the hall opened. Footsteps echoed through the room and now, underneath the rustle of lab coats and trousered legs, the metal casters on the floor. That could only mean the numbers would change. Someone new was being brought in.

The new person was installed in the room next door. She would be sleeping, whoever she was, her freshly shaved head gleaming under fluorescent lights. Her raw scalp would feel slightly numb at first. Then it would feel itchy. If she stayed in the hall for long enough, a researcher would come back and shave her head again, before the hair came back to disturb the cleanliness of her cell. Of course, she would be a woman. All specimens on this side of the hall were female. Opposite were males.

The researchers rustled back down the hall, the starched lab coats and footsteps the only movement in the place. When they got to the door F154 held her breath. She felt everyone in their glass cells striving in unison to hear the tiny click as it unlatched and opened to the outside world. Not an eye blinked, not a breath was taken, as each pair of ears strained to hear some whisper from beyond the door. What was outside? A hallway? An office? A lab?

F154 imagined the door opened onto a green field, doused in a bright white light. The sky was cellophane blue and there was a wide tree on the crest of a hill. Dandelions dotted the grass and insects droned between them. She wanted to walk over to the tree, it cast a deep shade underneath its branches and she could see buttress roots creating nooks against the cool earth.

She lay down in the shade, resting her head against the bark; its leaves whispered gently to her. She spoke to the tree, stroking its dry trunk with her fingertips. She didn't realise she had fallen asleep until the tree started to tell her its story. It told her about hundreds of years, its branches growing out into the world, the loss each autumn of its leaves and the excitement each spring as the tiny new ones grew from yellow buds into strong wide palms open to the sky. F154 wanted to hear more but the sedatives in her IV had taken her and she was lost to herself.

Valerie woke slowly. The world took a long time to come into focus. Her eyes seemed controlled from a long way away. She was in a white room; for a moment she assumed she was back in the cell. But looking around she realised she could see further than the four paces the cell afforded. Turning her head she saw medical equipment. She sat up and looked down at herself, still in blue scrubs, an IV drip in her arm and leading up to a bag hanging from a pole on wheels. There were wires attached to her chest. A catheter bag strapped to her thigh. Fear writhed in the pit of her stomach. She ran her hand along her shorn scalp, exploring the horror of her newly exposed skin, the reality of her confinement. Panic started to finger through her mind.

She wheeled the IV stand around the room, exploring its margins and its cool impassive walls. Within 15 minutes, she felt she knew everything there was to know about her tiny glass prison. On the other side of the glass to her right was another patient, a woman. Her head was shaved like her own and she wore identical scrubs. But her arms and legs were pale, her face was like a carving in stone. Her eyes were hollows in her bald head, dark and deep, her lids lowered. Was she watching? Valerie raised her hand in greeting. No response.

She had worked for the Corporation for two years but had never seen a facility like this, the row of glass rooms, each with their own sad occupant. They could be reflections of each other. Two mirrors face to face, reflecting the same misery back until the end of time. She counted four reflections, five including herself, with an identical set of glass rooms on the other side of the hall. They contained men, the same shaved heads bulbous atop their bodies.

The glass rooms were sealed, with vents in the glass ceiling, ducts carrying air snaked along the roof, meeting at the same point at the far end of the hall. The quiet hum of machinery, a gentle purring, made the room feel as though it were in the belly of some electronic animal. The air was cool and somehow tense, the medical instruments clicked over quietly, measuring her heart rate, blood pressure, output and input. She wrapped her arms around herself, a shiver taking hold. The concrete floor was cold under her bare feet. She went back to the hospital bed, clambered on it, brought her knees up to her chin and wrapped her arms around her legs.

An hour passed. And then another. Valerie shed silent tears, rocking herself back and forward, until there were no more tears to be shed. Finally she sat blankly wondering what would happen to her. There was a tangible sense of waiting in the room, she felt it from the woman in the room next to her, from the man opposite, who was now pacing, slowly dragging the IV stand along with him on its tiny wheels. Eventually, with a small click audible only because the entire room strained to hear it, the door at the end of the hall opened and two people in white lab coats walked up the corridor between the rows of glass rooms. A woman, her eyes on the clipboard in her hand, and a man, slipping a device into his lab coat pocket. They walked briskly to the door of Valerie's cell, footsteps like gunshots through the hall, and stood there. The woman looked up and met Valerie's gaze with her own calm expression.

"You are healthy," she said. "Your samples have been revealed to be suitable for further study. You will remain here. Our research teams will have access to you for samples around the clock. You are expected to comply with their requests. It is for the good of the Complex, and indeed the city, that you allow them to do their work unencumbered. Do you understand?"

Valerie blinked. She looked from the woman to the man and back again.

"Where am I?" she said.

"You are in the Complex. You are the property of the research teams. Your specimen number is F162. Do you understand?"

"My number? Why am I here? I called for a trial..." Valerie's voice was cracking through her panic.

The woman glanced at the man by her side and he took out his device and punched the screen several times with a stubby finger. A jolt of electricity coursed through Valerie's body, her muscles stiffened and coiled, and stopped. She was left gasping.

"Do you understand?" the woman said evenly.

"I demand to see The Director! There was to be a trial."

Another shock, a longer one, Valerie convulsed on her side on the bed.

"Do you understand?"

Valerie couldn't find her voice, it was stuck somewhere deep down inside her, beyond her reach.

"Do you understand?"

"Yes," Valerie whispered.

The woman and the man turned abruptly and marched back down the hall, as the doorway filled with people clad in ventilated clean suits. Their faces were invisible behind their masks.

Chapter Sixteen

David Newlin was at his monitor in the still of his office, behind his lab. A citywide shutdown had drawn most researchers out into the cafeteria, to watch rolling coverage from the Corporation's communications team. Residents on both sides of the Complex wall were assured they were being kept inside for their own safety, that the curfew would be lifted soon. But sitting at his monitor, alone, with only the rattle of the lab rats in their cages for company, David sniffed at the Corporation story. He scanned the security reports for Valerie. Surely the daughter of a researcher couldn't be detained and made an example of? But as he scanned information available at his clearance level it looked like she had disappeared. She had requested a trial, then the leak had happened. His daughter's face speaking out loud secrets the Corporation would kill to keep. Or worse. The only report after that point was that the person responsible was in custody. Custody meant she was alive. In theory.

David wasn't supposed to know about the secure sections, but the data he was expected to work with had to come from somewhere. And then there were the secrets Sarah had refused to keep. He tried not to think too much about it, put it to the back of his mind and remembered he was working for the greater good. He was saving lives. Or he would, eventually. Now, as he scrolled through the week's data, he looked for the location of each entry, hoping to see some kind of pattern form. But he was distracted, his mind flitting to that last email his wife had sent before the sudden illness took her words. *People need to know.* Valerie had sounded so like her. He couldn't lose them both.

He was about to give up when his eyes landed on a communication, this time from a device in Medical, demanding assistance transporting a patient to the 25th floor. The secure compound had been built with 12 underground levels; some of those levels, including David's own workspace in medical, had been divided and sectioned to accommodate an ever-growing number of functions. But how could there be 13 floors David knew nothing about?

David's pulse leapt into a gallop, as his body protested the realisation, his muscles and stomach felt heavy, pinning him to his chair. The medical data he was working with. Always new test subjects, all numbered and randomised. He ran a hand through his thinning hair and exhaled, forcing his breathing to slow, trying to clear the adrenalin fog. Valerie was right, if there were human test subjects held against their will, there could be hundreds of them. Maybe thousands. Involuntarily, David's eyes went to the cold store, where samples from the day's work were stored. The new cell smears and blood samples that had arrived that afternoon. Awaiting tomorrow's analysis. Tomorrow a new series would arrive. David, the researcher, would receive them on a trolley from a lab technician, he would sign his name next to them. He shuddered.

Like a sleepwalker, David went to the cold storage, and gazed at the new samples. Stored, numbered, no hint of personality or the cost borne to provide them. He took out a swab and, from the inside of his cheek, took cells containing his own DNA. A sample. He put it through the usual process, and into the machine, feeling the bile forcing its way up his throat as the screen showed a similarity. A female specimen. A blood relative.

Where had they put her? What had they done with her?

His hands shook as he took his security pass, and his jacket from his desk. His shock gave him a sense of detachment. He walked down the hall, managed to smile at a passing colleague, without engaging any conscious thought at all. His family, his own blood, providing cell samples for his tests. He felt as if he'd been fed a plate of human fingernails. It was easier to not think about it, but he'd always known, in the pit of his stomach, he knew those samples were human. He knew they'd been obtained illegally. The veneer of respectability had been so thin, just a glaze of paperwork and a dusting of process. Anyone who had not known was only in the dark because they'd willed it so. *People need to know*. He fought a wave of nausea and gritted his teeth.

"David!"

Chris, the research assistant. His voice followed him down the hall, its echoes swelling in the small space.

Footsteps coming from behind him. David ran a quick hand over his face, drawing off the layer of sweat. He clenched his teeth and drew his face into what he hoped was a neutral expression before he turned.

"Glad I caught you, they have a new series coming up for us from down below later today," Chris said, breathless. "Jesus, David, you OK?" He took a step back slightly, as though needing greater space to asses David's state.

David shrugged and faked a smile. "Long day," he said. "Lockdown doesn't help."

"Tell me about it," Chris visibly relaxed. "Anyway, I thought I'd better let you know. Viral affected tissue samples coming up, rush job apparently."

David blinked, staring blankly at the man. Another set of samples had never been delivered so quickly.

"Strange times we're living in, I guess they want to get some answers to give them out there." Chris jerked his head over his shoulder, as though the city's population was crowding the corridor behind him.

"Who gave you the notification?"

"Came through from Russell Smart's lab."

Smart's lab was beyond the secure section, need-to-know only research. He had never been told where the infected samples came from, but now he thought about it, he realised he'd never asked. He stood transfixed in the corridor, heart beating fast, as he wondered if Valerie's sample would be infected with the virus. It seemed beyond imagining. His senses felt numbed as he nodded to Chris.

"Anyway," Chris was already turning to walk away. "Maybe go

get a coffee or something, eh? You look like shit."

"Thanks. Will do."

Smart's lab was on the lowest floor of the secure Complex. He had no way in but if samples were transferred from Medical, perhaps he wouldn't need one. He stepped into the lift as though in a dream, thumbed the button with a shaking hand. Would the samples be human? Would they still be part of a whole person, flesh and blood? His flesh and blood? His limbs felt a long way away as he waited for the lift to reach the medical floor. But somewhere, deep in the back of his mind, dread was building, as solid and dark as a stormfront.

The longer Ava was in her cell, left to the timeless, soundless white room, the more it became her reality. She had no idea how long she had been there when the door finally opened, behind it a woman in scrubs and a surgical mask who stood by a wheeled stretcher.

Ava stared at the woman, who met her gaze with an expectant look. The stretcher sat between them, huge in the small room, an unspoken resolution to the silent standoff. *Do not get on that bed.* Ava was gripped by the thought. *Never.* Eventually though, the woman stepped back from the doorway and nodded sharply at someone Ava couldn't see. She knew she had nowhere to run but she backed away from the security man who approached regardless.

He sealed a meaty fist around one of her upper arms, but

couldn't catch the other as she windmilled, resisting with everything she had. She took her opportunity, smashing the heel of her free hand into his face. She felt a satisfying crunch and the white room blossomed with a splash of bright red blood as he released her, bringing his hands up in shock. She looked up, ready to vault for the door, a shoulder to the solar plexus of the woman in the mask—but the researcher was already on her other side, syringe in hand. The security man reached out a bloodied hand and curled it tight around her throat. She was pinned, chin tilted towards the ceiling, swallowing hard, as the researcher slipped the syringe into her vein.

"Why do they always have to make this so difficult?" the woman muttered through her mask.

The syringe slipped out and the hand around Ava's neck dropped her. She coughed once, and pushed resistant limbs towards the door, But the world had tilted, the linoleum stuck to her bare feet, each step a lingering struggle, before Ava's vision filled with the floor rising up to meet her. The impact was lost to the drug in her veins. She splashed, freefall, into her subconscious.

Something shifted around her, some change in pressure or pitch. Hard hands gripped her upper arms and calves, lifted her, then put her down again. She heard a voice, stretching into her sedation, long and sinuous. It wavered around her. She etched her eyes open, and focused, with some effort, on the figures standing around where she now lay on the stretcher. A man there, lab coat and ID card, in deep conversation with the researcher. The idea of escape drifted up to her from the deep blue, but her eyelids were rock solid weights, her limbs would not obey her commands. As she struggled to keep the people standing above her in focus, the man in the lab coat lurched out, in slow motion, striking the woman, who promptly disappeared from Ava's view. She closed and opened her leaden eyelids slowly, trying to make sense of the face that leaned over her. He was speaking but Ava could only catch every second word.

"Who....move..." The words billowed around her, without direction or purpose, "...walk..." A hand was at behind her shoulders propping her up, sliding her legs off the stretcher, she hung there half on and half off for a moment before the floor reached up and plucked her out of the air, pulling her down. A blink and she was up again, the man's arm around her waist, her feet trailing uselessly along the linoleum. "Help...." His words were bubbles floating in a miasma of sedation, popping with urgency around her. She became loosely aware that behind them, security men were giving chase. Shouts echoed through the corridor, words pulsed, their meaning lost. She grappled with the sedation, tried to take control of her limbs, pressed back against the floor as it reached out to suck her legs down again. The corridor lengthened, perspective pulling it together at the ends, stretching it out like vertigo.

She had no idea how many tortured steps she'd managed to coax out of her legs when the man stopped walking. She looked up to see a locked door in front of her. She felt the man jostling her weight, propping her against the wall of the corridor and looking at her with desperate, searching eyes.

"I. Will. Open. It," he said, each word punctuated the sedative bubble. "Can. You. Get. Through?"

Ava nodded hazily. The man disappeared from her field of vision and she sank down against the wall, dragged herself against the door, and lay there panting. In the corridor they'd come through, a security man stalked her slowly, weapon drawn. Behind him she could still see the hospital bed, though it had felt they'd walked for miles. The woman researcher sat on it, surgical mask gone, blood drenching the front of her scrubs, a shout in the pristine white corridor. She focused on the blood, on the brightness of sudden pain, quick release, and as she did the door disappeared behind her and she fell into the corridor on the other side.

The world slipped out of the slow motion of the drugs in her system, the security man approached at a run and the other man, the stranger, appeared above her. She scrabbled on the slick floor, fighting inertia, a leaden gravity that affected her alone. Her bare feet slipped. She fought, gripped the wall on the other side of the door frame and hefted her hips through, her lower legs and feet still lingering in the corridor, still prey for the security man who was there, he was on her, his gun was drawn, she paused, the world narrowed to only his eyes, the hatred there, the single-minded intent of stopping her, stopping her dead, she was dead, her legs would not obey her command and she was dead.

Then the man, the stranger, was above her, hands under her armpits pulling her, sliding her, wrestling her. A tortured screaming voice filled the corridor and Ava realised it was coming from inside her, her mouth was open and she was screaming; her feet were still in the corridor the security man's head bobbed around as he searched for a clean shot. The man gave her one final shove, her feet passed through the door and it slid closed like a blink. He staggered and fell onto her, a knee in her abdomen registering from a very long way away, and the hall was filled with their own ragged breathing. The coil in her spine sent tendrils of pain through her, electric shocks along her bones.

The lift he dragged her into had a security card slot but only carried buttons to the 10th floor. They travelled as far as they could on it, stepped out and slipped into a storage cupboard. The man slid her onto the ground and leaned against the wall himself, both struggling to catch their breath. Ava realised he was not a young man.

"I'm David," he said.

"Ava."

He nodded.

Time passed. Ava thought the man left, and returned, she wasn't sure if she slept. In time, she sat up and the haziness had gone. The man had left a pair of plastic clogs and a lab coat on the floor next to her.

Dressed, she emerged from the storeroom into another corridor. This one was dimly lit. An extension in the secure section of the Complex, a fresh dip into the surrounding rock. The walls were bare concrete, the scent of the earth surrounding her was tangible. She could almost feel the grit on her tongue. This was a new area, she could tell, home to Corporation secrets. Kept close, deep underground.

She had no idea what she intended to do, but she knew she had to do something. She didn't know how to reach the surface, but even if she did she couldn't simply walk away. She felt herself involved now, tied to this horror by the hardware embedded in her spine. She wandered, searching for the man who had pulled her out of whatever research the Corporation had planned for her. They had done this to her without her permission. She wanted to break something. The rage that flowed through her was ordered somehow, funnelled in a way that made her calm and focussed. All her life she'd watched things fall apart. She'd watched the loss, one by one, of her family. A constant futile attempt to catch her life like fine sand running through her fingers. It wasn't fair that she had never had a permanent home, that she'd been mistreated and used. It wasn't fair that she had lost Sophia, the light to her shade, the person who kept her kind, who kept her human. It wasn't fair that now she had been altered. She wanted to take control.

She found David behind a terminal in a small security office. He sat in the dark, the light from the screen catching the crevices on his face, ageing him beyond years. He turned towards her as she walked in and surveyed her quietly. No doubt he had as many questions about her as she had about him.

"They did something to me." It just fell out. She was at such a loss for where to start, it didn't seem to matter. David just raised his eyebrows.

"They did something to my spine."

His eyes drifted down her slim frame, confusion giving way to curiosity. Ava slid the lab coat off, let it drop to the floor, turned and raised the back of the surgical scrub shirt she was wearing. There, in her lower back. It was something nameless, something not-Ava. Ava stood as David's featherlight fingertips inspected her. There was something embedded there, and a small protrusion. Deep inside her, underneath the revulsion, she could feel its tiny coil. And rather than weaken her, somehow it reinforced her resolve. If she could survive this she could survive anything.

"Can you remove it?" she asked.

"No." David's voice was quiet.

She turned to face him again. His eyes carried a grief, a horror, for which she was unprepared.

"But I think I know who can," he said.

Chapter Seventeen

They sat together, sharing a few quiet words, under the earth, under stone undisturbed for eons, until humanity had asked it to hide its secrets and wipe its collective hands clean. David explained his search for the restricted access labs where Ava had been destined. Ava couldn't help but think he would have had better luck if he'd left her to her fate, and followed her trail. She glanced at him out of the corner of her eye, trying to read the stranger who had, for reasons of his own, saved her life.

Along the wall, a series of security readouts glowed quietly in the dark. A scrolling stream of ingress and egress, from people to equipment. Even the air vents were tracked, monitored. As they sat there a red box flashed up on the screen, blinked rhythmically for thirty seconds before disappearing. Ava tapped David's shoulder and gestured with her chin.

"The exhaust fan," David said. "There's an upper pressure limit. It vents every now and again. Nothing unusual."

As soon as the words escaped his lips, he turned to stare at the readouts. His expression turned from despair to curiosity. He exited out of the search window he was in and briskly navigated elsewhere through the labyrinthine system. His shoulders tensed up and his head craned into the monitor, lips pressed tight together.

"Here's the ventilation system," he said eventually. "But here's another ventilation system. Who would go to the trouble of building two sets of ducts?"

In the white space of Ava's mind, the underground warren turned into a network of air conditioning vents, fibre optic cables, server banks and gas exchanges. All those pipes and tubes sending air and electronic messages into its depths.

"Someone with a lot to hide, mate," she said.

As David read out the data, Ava sketched a picture of the extra 13 floors. There were eight floors of living quarters. Totally secure and seemingly rarely used. The other floors were constantly active, the lights never switched off. It had its own ventilation system, its own power supply.

"There has to be a way to get her out," David said under his breath.

"Her?"

"My daughter." He turned back to the monitor. "I thought you were her, when I went looking for you in Medical."

"But you work for them. Why would they have your daughter?"

"She stole something."

Ava's skin crawled. Valerie. And she was lost, hidden in the bowels of the complex. *You think everyone in the resistance isn't loved by someone?*

"Was the broadcast released?" Ava whispered. "The information she had?"

David turned to face her and stared as though seeing her for the first time.

"How did you know?"

"I met Valerie, in the city. I helped her get the message out. Wherever she is, I'm supposed to be there too."

The earth rocked Valerie to sleep, long and deep, in her cell. A part of her, the part that knew she would never see the sky again, understood the IV gave her a sedative. But another part felt the depth of her glass cage, felt the earth around her. The rock sang ancient dreams, and she floated with it. Time drifted, long time, geological time. In her dreams flittered small fish, and later sharks, emerging silently out of the deep, and away again. As she slept the earth held her, pressed up against her tight. She felt small and big at the same time, she, who had walked the crust of the planet and lain down to sleep along its bones, kept warm by its marrow and nourished by its beating heart.

Ava carried David's security pass with her, but after the assault on the researcher in medical she doubted it would be any use. No doubt security were searching for him now, too. The pair had done all they could via the control panels, and had split up to cover more ground. But now they knew where they were going they both felt the urgency, the knowledge that every moment that passed was taking Valerie that little bit further away. Ava tried not to touch anything, David had urged her to leave no trace. Even his every key stroke was being recorded somewhere, logged along with the ventilation pressures and the vital signs of patients in Medical.

She slipped into one of the labs and looked around, unable to make sense of the equipment. Her whole life she had been moving from one wrecked place to another; she had run from disease, from rape, from starvation. She had never been in a place so clean and orderly. It made her feel exposed, as though she were a stain on the pristine walls. In the far corner of the room was a walk-in refrigerator. She tried the security card and the door hissed open, an exchange of gasses and blast of cold air leaking out into the lab as she slipped inside. Inside were shelving units, stacked with equipment, and a secure cabinet in a far corner. Wielding an unknowable metal instrument, it took all of Ava's strength but the door burst open. She snatched handful of vials from inside the cabinet, slipped them in the pocket of her lab coat, with a couple of syringes. She had no idea what was in the vials. Could be a disease, could be a cure. Whatever it was, it was worth locking up. She walked with renewed confidence, feeling armed.

She knew where she was going, down to the bottom, as far as she could. The security breach David had triggered remotely had been logged as a fire. All the locked doors would be unlocked, a gasp to allow staff to escape. The lower floor would flood with security, like antibodies with rushing in to cauterise the wound. Her window of opportunity would be brief.

She swapped elevators at the 12th floor. The security shaft was hidden behind a maintenance panel as David had surmised, the elevator murky in emergency lighting. She rode the elevator as far as it went and stepped out into a bright and busy corridor. The flow of people around her was mixed—security, researchers—all with an urgent need to be somewhere else. The worry was tangible in the air, an acrid feeling that caught the back of her throat. But it hadn't given way to panic. Even now, 25 storeys underground, they had a job to do.

She knew she was looking for Hall 5, but what that meant was anyone's guess. She walked purposefully, trusting her lab coat, her businesslike air would blend into the general movement. At a security station she spoke to a guard.

"I need to get samples before lockdown, usually I'd send a runner but it's crazy right now, can you point me in the right direction?" It was risky, but there was no other way.

The security man glanced at his tablet, wide-eyed, and jerked his head down a corridor without even looking at her.

"On your right, you can't miss it," he said.

She slipped away without a word, thankful for woefully ill-prepared Scylla security for the first time. The corridor he had sent her down was quiet, and on the right-hand side another security post outside an airlock was manned by a serious looking security team. She fingered the syringe, full of whatever was in the stolen vials, wondering if it was time. Could she bluster her way through? Tucking the syringe up her sleeve she rearranged herself, drew herself up tall. After days in a cell, she looked intense. She looked like a woman with nothing to lose. In the barely restrained chaos, perhaps that would be enough.

She approached the security post at a brisk pace. The security men looked up, uninterested, as she kept walking without slowing down. She nodded at one of them, but his eyes already had a question forming. Shit, Ava thought. Nothing's ever easy.

"Aren't you forgetting something, doctor?" the man asked her, jabbing his chin towards a tablet monitor on the desk in front of him.

Ava shook her head, as if to clear it, and gave him a sheepish smile.

"Lost in my thoughts, what with the lock down," she said. She looked at the monitor. It asked for a log in. She brought up her right hand to type into the tablet, shot an embarrassed look at the security man.

"Could you give me a hand? I've lost my glasses," she said. She slipped the syringe from her sleeve.

He walked around to the other side of desk. Put his hands on either side of the tablet.

"Sure, what's your code?"

Ava grabbed his arm, turning him. Held the syringe tight against his throat. Against the skin, but not puncturing it.

"This is one of the most deadly specimens in the lab," she said between gritted teeth. "Tell your friend to stand down."

The security guard stood stiff, eyes wide, and told his partner to sit, hands on the table.

"Now tell him to put his gun and communicator on the floor and slide them to me," Ava said.

The security man did as he was told. Ava kicked both out of their reach.

"Lie face down on the floor, hands on your head."

Keeping the syringe against the security man's throat she slipped his gun out of its holster and put it in her coat pocket. She did the same with his communicator. She moved deliberately and slowly, making sure she controlled the situation. She wanted them all to pay.

She urged him to the ground and forced them to shuffle back down the corridor, to the first door she saw. A storeroom.

"You," she nodded at the man closest to it. "Open it."

When they were inside she closed them in and brought the grip of the handgun down on the handle, hard, once, twice, until the aluminium shifted under the impact.

Pocketing the second gun, she still had no idea what she would do. But if that's where Valerie was, she needed to get inside. And whatever was in there, she wanted to break it.

Outside the door to the hall was an air lock. She used her security card on the door, it opened with a pneumatic hiss, and she stepped into a bright, white light.

Looking around, blinking, she saw a large room full of smaller glass cubicles. At the far end, inside one of the cubicles she saw people in yellow clean suits. They hadn't seen her yet. They clustered around someone else, a subject, Ava guessed, a subject with a shaved head, dressed in blue scrubs identical to her own. The researchers were intent about their work. They had plastic briefcases with them, filtered air being pumped into their suits.

Ava watched, slipping the gun into her lab coat pocket, keeping her hand on it. In the glass rooms, were the bowed, shaven heads of other people. Dressed identically, adopting the same hyper awareness, she could feel them listening to her movements, she could feel their guardedness, their eyes that missed nothing even as they were lowered. She stepped silently between the two rows of sealed glass rooms, looking around her at their inhabitants, their medical equipment quietly ticking, monitoring their every heartbeat, the ebb and flow of their bodies as they quietly respired.

And then it costs you everything.

Something was very wrong in this room. She sensed fear in the glass cages, bowed heads and lidded eyes a picture of despair. She walked to the door to the last room in the hall, the one with the researchers inside and stopped, turning to face them. The door was closed and there was no keypad for her card. She wanted to break the glass, to destroy the walls keeping these people hostage. Prisoners inside their own bodies, bodies just vessels for the Scylla Corporation.

Slowly, deliberately, one of the suited researchers moved towards the door. A gloved hand stabbed at a handheld device and the door hissed open, there was another hiss as it closed behind the suited person. Closer now, Ava could see the face of a woman behind the mask, confusion clearly visible in her eyes.

"Who are you? This is a clean room," the woman said, her voice muffled behind the plastic.

She felt the gun under her hand, its cool certainty concealed in her pocket, and fought the urge to pull it out, threaten the woman, rip the mask off her face, to look her directly in the eyes. She took a moment to control her breathing, to let her wildest impulses pass.

"I'm an overseer taking over this shift, I've asked to get across all our operations down here," Ava said, hoping the bluff would sound convincing.

The woman's face crumpled in on itself as she frowned.

"This is a clean room, you can't be in here," she said. "The subjects are extremely sensitive."

Ava swallowed back bile. Adrenalin rushed through her veins, made it difficult for her to think clearly. She tried to keep her voice steady as she opened her mouth to respond. Instead movement in the cell to her left caught her eye. She saw a woman in there, shaved head like the other captives, same blue scrubs, same dark eyes. But something about the way she moved her head seemed familiar, some semi shrug that she recalled having seen on someone else. An anonymous subject wearing the skin that belonged to someone Ava had once met. Stepping around the researcher, Ava approached the glass wall of the cell. As she stood there, the woman turned her head. She didn't make eye contact, Ava couldn't be certain if she saw her at all. But it was Valerie. The same mild eyes, though now they were dim. Ava stared wide-eyed at the woman she had come to think of as a friend. Slowly Valerie lifted her eyes to meet Ava's. The two women exchanged an unspoken moment of recognition. Valerie's eyes broke contact with Ava's, they dropped to the same low lidded gaze at the floor. What had happened to Valerie in there?

She turned back to the researcher and squared her shoulders.

"Open this one," she said.

"I can't. You're not wearing a suit."

Ava drew the gun from her pocket.

"Open it."

The researcher's eyes went wide behind the face shield. She glanced from Ava's eyes to the gun several times and punched a few numbers on her device.

The door opened with the same pneumatic hiss, and Ava slipped inside. She rushed to Valerie and grabbed her by the shoulders, one hand on each side.

"Valerie," she hissed.

Valerie's eyes slowly drifted to meet Ava's. Almost unrecognisable. Except that half shrug. The way she held her shoulders loose and back, the way she moved through the world lightly, as though she was not quite a part of it. But behind her eyes was nothing but her glass cage.

"Valerie," she whispered. "I'm going to get you out of here."

There was no recognition in Valerie's eyes, but her head turned again, to look blankly at the woman in the glass cell next door. As she watched a woman in a cell four down the row came into view through the glass. She was pacing her room, making brief circuits from one side to the other, going out of view as she passed behind equipment.

Ava coursed with anger. She looked back to Valerie with searching eyes, looking for some recognition. The despair in Valerie's stance, the fear in her eyes and the downturn of her mouth, on her face that was always so ready to smile, made Ava's decision for her. She pulled Valerie close and holding the gun to her throat, walked her out of the glass room in front of her. Ava looked fiercely at the researcher who still stood outside the glass cell, stunned, the device in her hand long forgotten.

"Open the other cells," she said.

"These people are the property of Scylla, they can't go outside the cells," she said.

"Open them!"

"You won't get out of the Complex. You're 25 storeys underground." But the woman was already tapping at the device, looking up at the cells periodically. One by one they opened.

The researchers in the cell opposite were panicking, one of them on a device. Soon security men would rush into the room, Ava would not be put into a cell, she knew it, she would be shot on sight. The coil in her spine twitched in time with her racing pulse. A reminder. A threat.

She reached into her pocket and put the gun in Valerie's hand, closing her limp fingers around the handle. Valerie held it casually at waist height, levelled at the researcher standing in front of her. The subjects stirred as the doors opened. Now, a couple of men and a woman wandered the space between the cells. The woman in the cell next to Valerie's did not stir. She gazed blankly at the now opened cell door as though she had no idea she could walk through it. Her eyes flitted between the door and Ava's face and something deep in Ava's memory pined with recognition. Then, as the woman turned Ava saw. She saw in hideous colour the tattoo on her arm.

Valerie found her tongue. She shouted across the hall, wordlessly at first, her voice cracked and unused. Her shouts tarted to form the word 'move' but the women in the cell seemed unable to hear her. Ava watched as one man staggered, grabbing the glass walls, as though his frame could not support his weight. Another subject stopped by his side and took his shoulder gently. The researchers in their yellow suits stood stunned, didn't stop them as they walked out. They weren't soldiers. They weren't going to restrain anyone walking around.

It all passed by Ava as though in a nightmare, the people struggling to escape, the researchers looking around ineffectually and in the bright burning centre: her sister. Ava had an identical tattoo. A tall ship. They had got them together, when their sea voyage ended. They had been filled with loss but also gratitude to have survived. To still have each other.

Sophia stood looking back at her with hollowed out eyes. Lost, her eyes said. Ava felt it intensely. Lost to the Corporation, lost to the cell and the IV still attached to her arm. Lost to the cool earth surrounding them and the 25 storeys of excavation above. Lost to her own dreams. Ava gestured to her. *Come here.* Sophia, this altered Sophia who looked so much older than the woman Ava had lost, just shook her head in the smallest of movements. Her eyes shifting between Ava and the interior of her cell. The same look of knowing. Of being certain. That look of certainty that Ava knew to be so much a part of her sister. Sophia. Who was always so determined. Now paralysed with terror, unable to step through an open door.

It was as they stared at each other, two sisters separated only by fear, that Russell Smart and the Director entered the room. Ava barely registered the new presence until Valerie let out a shout.

"You'd lock us up like this? Is this nature taking its course?"

The Director met Valerie's eyes but Russell was focused on Ava.

"So you're the one who's been causing our security teams so much trouble," he said evenly. "The researcher you maimed was one of our best, you should know."

Ava looked at Valerie, hoping for some explanation. This was her world, after all. Ava was used to the subterfuge of the streets, the way you washed coins in vinegar each night, the way you avoided the attention of street thugs. But this political intrigue? She had no patience for it. She wasn't a game player, she was a survivor. She moved towards the woman still in the cell, the woman who used to be Sophia.

"You can't keep people here like this," Valerie said, in a monotone, fist clenching the gun like a lifeline.

"Actually, we can. And we have," Russell responded.

He gestured at Sophia, whose eyes were locked on Ava's, still inside the cell.

"See Valerie?" he said. "People are frightened. When people are scared they need someone to take charge. When the Government collapsed that was us. People need us. Even when we hurt them, they want us to be in control. They'd rather we were in control than no-one."

Valerie didn't answer. It was as if Sophia had never considered the door might one day open and release her.

Ava stood outside Sophia's glass cell, unwilling to walk inside, unwilling to leave. Her eyes widened when the doors to all the cells automatically closed. An alarm sounded through the hall and one by one, a red panel appeared on each door mechanism on the cells. It seemed to cut through the fear and stir Sophia into reaction. She looked up and down the long hall, before running forward, pressed herself against the door, each line on her palms showing clearly through the glass. One for life. One for love. Ava lifted her hands and mirrored her sister's stance, meeting her palms against the glass. Their shared history flowed between them, the bond of sisters. Finally, when each cell door carried a red panel there was a moment's silence, somehow more terrifying than the alarm had been. A silence in which everyone in the room heard their own heartbeat, loud and fast.

"Open it," Ava yelled at the researcher.

The woman just shook her head.

"Open it!" She screamed, her eyes filling with tears.

A gentle exhaust hiss came from the ventilation ducts on top of each cell. Sophia looked up, then straight at Ava, and choked as the poison found its way into her lungs. She collapsed, spasming, while the researchers with their sealed suits and compressed air canisters stood impassively in the now empty cell at the end. The final research subject eventually lay still on the floor of her cell and one by one the red panel on each door went blank.

Ava's hands dropped and she leaned her whole body along the glass, her muscles unwilling to hold her upright. She crumpled to the floor, bringing both hands to her face. Valerie moved forward on bare feet, and reached down to her shoulder.

"Don't touch me!" Ava yelled. She struggled to her feet, steadying herself along the glass wall, tears streaking its surface. Ava turned to face Russell, with a twisted expression.

"You didn't even know her name," she said, tears making her throat thick and clumsy. "Her name was Sophia."

"She didn't have a name," Russell responded. "That makes it easier for us all."

"You're inhuman." Valerie pulled Ava towards her.

"Perhaps. But we're fighting to save humanity."

Russell gestured around at the researchers, the glass cells, the subjects. They all stood motionless, a tableau of hunter and hunted. "We're fighting for survival. We're the only ones who can."

"This isn't survival," Valerie spat back.

"Perhaps it's best to think of it as evolution," Russell said.

"I don't want it."

"Yes. Well. We can accommodate that, of course," Russell answered. "We avoid termination of a test wherever we can. But sometimes we need to cut our losses." He nodded towards Sophia's motionless body.

Somewhere, deep in the panels and hallways of the underground warren, a siren started to scream. A persistent, mechanical sound, predating the gas and the glass cells, it pierced the inertia. All around them the researchers and security men, even Russell himself, dove instinctively for their communicators.

"The flood alarm!" Russell barked. "The city's breached!" He glanced at Valerie and Ava with wide eyes.

"Deal with them," he muttered to the security detail behind him. Then into his communicator: "Report to the Complex wall. We have incoming."

He turned and rushed from the room. The Director paced forward, slowly, deliberately, to stand in front of Ava.

"You're braver women than I have ever been," she said in a voice torn from her very marrow. She gripped Ava's hands in her own. "I'm sorry for your loss."

Chapter Eighteen

The world slipped into tense slow-motion as Ava backed out of the hall. Focused on another emergency, Russell paused when he realised the Director wasn't with him. The woman remained where she stood, hands still in front of her, eyes fixed on Ava's retreat. Russell gave a curt nod to one of the security guards as he left the room. The guard raised his gun and casually fired into the Director's skull. Her eyes widened into sudden surprise for an instant, then her body pitched forward and crumpled, as though the puppeteer had grown tired of her. Fate hesitated for an excruciating moment as the security man's eyes flicked from the Director's body to Ava. She braced, resigned to her death, insensible from Sophia's awful choking. When the gunshot rang out she jumped and watched the security man collapse as though from a long way away. She turned to see Valerie lowering her gun. She was yelling but the sounds made no sense. Valerie stepped forward and shook Ava roughly.

"We've got to run!"

The tension broke; the pair turned and ran from the room and down a corridor that seemed unending, far longer than any Ava had seen underground so far. They ran alongside the people from the glass cells. From time to time one of the other subjects would fall, each time she grabbed them under the arms as quickly as she could, barely breaking pace as she hauled them to their feet. The alarm though. That was everywhere. As they ran, doors on either side started opening. Out of them staggered blank looking people. Men, women, Ava even spotted a child. Shaved, wearing scrubs, barefoot. Their group paused as they saw the newcomers, confusion momentarily outweighing the urge to escape.

"Run!" Ava yelled, barely breaking her stride to pick up a child who looked barely six years old. "Run!"

It was all she could do, the wire in her spine complained as her muscles ached. Every cell in her body was screaming run. She echoed the thought herself, yelling at everyone around her. "Run!" Eventually security would seal the lower levels. They had to get to the stairwell or be locked inside.

Ava couldn't tell how many prisoners there were, the panic and grief clouding her eyes made it seem she had always been running. She started to hear the beating of bare feet as a kind of rhythm, a river slamming against rocks in its path, forcing her forwards. She was running with a herd of humanity. But ahead a bottleneck started to form. People had stopped. She pushed her way forward, trying to force them on, shouting and begging and threatening. The people looked at her blankly. Could they not hear? Could they not speak? Why would they stand there waiting for death? The vision of Sophia's lifeless eyes filled her mind. Finally, ahead she saw a wall. Barely finished after it was hewn out of the rock, it was solid, impenetrable and a dead end. There was a door in it, standing closed, electronic lock with a blank control panel. The door to the old evacuation stairwell. Ava tested the door with an experimental hand. It held firm. David. Perhaps he hadn't been able to trip the system. Perhaps he had been shot.

She put down the child she was carrying and took big gulping, ragged breaths, her fist pounding on the door, wishing she could obliterate the Complex with her bare hands. She wanted publicity, she wanted honesty. She wanted a witness to this horror that had all been for nothing. She wanted the world to grieve for her sister. *Ignorance is cheap Ava*, she heard Sophia's voice in her head, *and then it costs you everything.*

The alarm filling the air around them went abruptly silent. Then, in the deafening void that followed, Ava heard the tiny sound of the electronic lock opening. She turned to the door and gently pushed it. It gave a click as it opened for the first time in years and, old hinges howling in protest, the door slowly inched open.

Ava and the child next to her straightened their spines simultaneously and exchanged a wordless glance. And the herd moved forward.

They climbed. The stairs were solid steel, set into the rock. It was dark, and the only light was creeping through the ever more distant corridor they had left. They went slowly, being certain of each footfall, ensuring no-one tripped or was left behind on a landing. There was no leader of the group. It was subject to its own fits and whims, its own mysterious needs and fears. There was no individual ambition; Ava could only travel with it, hoping for safety in its multitudes, praying not to stumble. The herd stepped and panted as one, the stairwell filling with animalistic sweat scent of flight. There was a uniformity of footfall on each stair, hands groping in the dark for railings or for rock wall, eyes weeping, and hearts beating loudly. Breath growing faster as the climb drew on. But the herd could only go forward, so climb on it did.

Gradually, imperceptibly at first, a hint of grey appeared in the darkness. Ava realised she could see the shaved heads of people in front of her, then she could see the walls of the stairwell, then she could see the stairs themselves. Looking around she could see the mass of humanity she was now part of—living, sweltering, dark eyes shining in the half light. Light was coming from somewhere. There was a door, or a ventilation shaft. An escape. But rounding the corner the herd came to a standstill. Shoving her way forward, she looked for the source of the blockage.

Bars. There was a door—it stood wide open. But the doorway was sealed by steel bars, a gate, rusted, old, but solid. Ava gripped them, one in each hand. Turning to look beyond the bars, she was surprised to recognise where she was. Outside the stairwell she saw the night-time marketplace, the flood water still lingering in puddles from a week ago. There were no people around. The moon shone bright overhead and the marketplace was nearly silent, the earth seemed poised for some reckoning, some sudden realisation. Bats circled a big tree beyond the market and somewhere, from further away, movement. Not voices, nothing they could identify. The sound of tree branches breaking, stone on stone, metal on metal.

"Hello!" Her voice reverberated at wild angles, back into the stairwell, and across the marketplace. Just a stone's throw away would be the first of the wet suburbs on the northern shore, just a block or two beyond that would be the ferry stand, the fisherman's boats that never sleep on a still night like this. The river should have been teeming with people and by extension, the market. There should have been people cooking, street kids lingering in the shadows, commuters making their way to and from the river. Fear started to burn Ava's muscles like lactic acid, gnawing at her resolve. She had expected riots, she had expected protests and people storming the gates of the Complex. Humanity was good at making noise. It was never good at being quiet. Not this quiet.

"There!" Valerie shouted.

As she watched, the darkness congealed into shapes. The silence in the night air grew deeper and turned into the sound of listening. And eventually, she heard it, an unmistakable shuffle. Soft feet, bare or in plastic sandals and sneakers, moving through the square, at the edges. In the shadows. The sound was soft and rustling but seemed to surround them. A gust of wind buffeted the square, throwing open a shutter somewhere, and a shaft of light fell across the market.

In it, Ava saw the shadows of hundreds of people, elongated by the angle of the light, stretching through the tents and shanties. They ducked and weaved as their owners moved forward, down the street. She swallowed hard and stared, barely breathing, as a line of people, ordinary people, made its way through the market. She watched their firm grip on weapons. Scythes, fishing spears, even more than a few rifles. They took slow, but determined steps, until someone at the front lifted his hand in a signal and they stopped. She watched the leader's arm, held up in a fist, tendrils of a long tribal tattoo clinging to it. A few beats went by before she realized she wasn't breathing.

Next to her Valerie squeezed her hand tight, somewhere behind her someone had started to moan. These people wouldn't be able to hold it together much longer, they would panic, and panic in the herd could kill. She shifted down to examine the gate in front of her.

"A lock," Ava said to Valerie next to her. "A handle, anything."

They groped through the dark and there, in a shadow, covered in rust was a small padlock. So simple.

Behind her Ava heard someone start to sob.

Up the street to the left, out of her field of vision came a noise Ava hadn't heard since childhood. An engine, a big one, making its way through the deserted city streets. Whoever was driving it was not familiar with such a machine either, the gears crunched loud as shotgun blasts in the night. Underneath the bellowing diesel, Ava could hear the crunch of booted feet. Lots of them. She started backing away from the bars with her arms out on either side of her, pushing the people around her back into the dark of the stairwell. The noise grew closer, and louder, until eventually security teams came into view. More than Ava had ever seen together. They were quiet, moving in rows as one towards the river. When the first Scylla men reached the market square the engine came into view. A hulking farm vehicle, wearing homemade armour, enormous tyres crushing community planted vegetable patches. The whole convoy stopped at the square and surveyed the scattered resisters. Ava held her breath, praying the people behind her, and all the way down however many flights of the stairwell they were crowded in, could stay quiet. She heard a quiet sob from behind her right shoulder and a shout from one of the security men. Her stomach sank.

But the security men weren't looking towards the stairwell. A few commands were exchanged by barking male voices and the Scylla teams moved, approaching with eyes straight ahead and steady, careful steps. As Ava watched, a shutter on an upstairs window of a building across the square opened and something, a dark shape, lit and smoking, was thrown out. Her mind stopped in confusion, as the object flew, turning in the air and leaving a trail of inky smoke, across the alleyway in front of the stairwell she stood in, making a neat arc, set to land almost at her feet. A shout went up among the Scylla crew.

"Get down!" Ava pulled Valerie by the arm, took a step back, and the blast threw her off her feet. The world blurred.

Dust filled the air and with a screech the gate gave way. She found herself on the floor, Valerie standing over her shouting something she couldn't hear. People were running. Staggering to her feet, she looked up. The iron bars ripped away, the stairwell bricks in rubble, barefoot test subjects scattered, disappearing into the dark.

Somewhere, someone screamed in pain.

Chapter Nineteen

Valerie had never so much as seen a punch thrown before this night.

Around her gunfire and shouts echoed through the square, a liquid violence that dispersed and reformed at intervals, punctuated by the shuffles and near silence of running feet. Somewhere across the square a fire had started.

Valerie stood bent at the hips, holding Ava around the waist, staying low in the shadows of the crumbling buildings behind her. She ground her teeth against the panic. Outside the stairwell the ground was covered in rubble, dotted with a handful of injured or dazed security men, walls threatening to fall. Beyond them, screams.

She gripped onto Ava, plotting out a route in between buildings, somewhere she could hide until dawn. Until whatever this was had ended. A hand settled on her shoulder from behind and a hot breath crept into her ear.

"Stay still," a voice whispered. Valerie's blood went cold. She stood, frozen to the spot, gripping onto Ava as if the woman's dazed form would save her life. A moment passed as a security man holding a rifle stormed past, murder in his eyes, heading to the river where the sounds of screams and gunfire still echoed.

As he passed the hand on Valerie's shoulder loosened. She leapt away, turning to look behind her.

"Are you injured?" Standing amid the ruins, looking as tidy as ever, was her dad. She stared.

"Valerie?"

Behind them a wall collapsed. More dust filled the air. Gunfire and the sounds of screams intensified.

"We need to get across the square. Help me with her," Valerie shouted.

They ran. Falling. Scrambling. Each with one arm around Ava's waist, they half walked, half carried her through the remains of the marketplace. Rubble was everywhere and they could hear voices coming from the ground around them. Shouts. Some for help. Some shouting names they didn't recognise. Some were wordless. They did not stop. They stepped out of the light, and ducked down a laneway. Sitting Ava down against a wall, they looked back out the way they came. There was the occasional flash and rumble of a homemade grenade in the distance.

Dawn was coming, and the sky in the east grew lighter. As the deep night sky silvered to grey, they saw running figures, silhouetted, carrying weapons, moving together. Valerie knew there had been a resistance, but she was stunned to see it in the light. The people, most of them young—too young—arming themselves with whatever they could. People would die at the end of Scylla rifles, which would only fan the anger. She watched the sun rise, knowing that whatever unstable truce she'd lived through was over.

There was another grenade flash, and the light from a fire burning in the distance intensified. The gunfire retreated, moving across the city, and became less frequent.

"It will be difficult in the City from now on," David Newlin said quietly. "The people won't back down. They won't believe anymore."

Valerie watched as the battle was won, thinking about the war that had only just started.

"People are resourceful. People are survivors," she said. Where had she heard that before?

"Whatever survives the next 100 years, it won't be this society," he said turning to her. "That's why we did it, that's why we took the offer to move into the Complex. This world isn't under our control Valerie. It isn't fit for humans. It is fit for fish and bats."

Valerie glanced back at the river and then looked her dad in the eye.

"Surviving doesn't mean becoming monsters," she said. "If it did there'd hardly be any point."

Tears filled her father's eyes.

"I know, my love," he said. He pulled her close and held her, resting his chin on her head. "I've always said we're lucky you use your powers for good."

David Newlin wasn't a warrior. He wasn't a freedom fighter. But he did believe he should take care of his family. He was old fashioned. He farewelled Valerie, promising to track her down in a few days. As the city picked itself up and dusted itself off in the dawn, he made his way back to the Complex, walking through the unmanned checkpoint at the front gate. All security were out defending the city, leaving the Complex to stand open, solar panels gleaming as the light grew.

He was determined to find Lucas, to make sure his foster son knew who he was working with. As far as he could tell, the system was a failed experiment. He needed to abort, record his observations, and move on. Some part of him felt he needed to give Lucas the chance to walk away.

Walking into his house he knew immediately something was wrong. He walked through to the kitchen and found, sitting at the table, Lucas Ngyuen and Russell Smart, flanked by two security men. David looked at their stony faces and realised he'd never really known his adopted son. The man he'd all but raised was a stranger. Lucas had been there through Sarah's illness, had sat by her bedside, stood alongside David and Valerie at Sarah's funeral. Lucas and David had sat together in the room that Sarah had lain in to the end. A room haunted by pain and grief, the things they might have wanted to say to each other now insignificant or too late. Such an ordinary thing, death. So everyday. They had sat in that empty room, newly bare of hospital equipment, and wordlessly grieved. Alone but together.

Now, David saw Lucas was a different man. He could see it in him, just by his posture, his ease with Russell, his assumption that the security men behind him were precisely where they should be. Lucas was changed in the look in his eye, the steady, confident gaze with which he pinned David to the spot. And he was changed by the handgun sitting on the table in front of him. The absolute surety in the room that he would use it.

"Hello, David," Russell said.

"Hello."

Lucas put both hands on the table, not looking at the weapon in front of him. David watched this new man take charge, dominate the room, his presence filling the air like a gas, fit to suffocate them all. He wondered if Lucas had known that Sarah's sickness was deliberately caused, even as he'd held her hand. Even as he'd watched her die.

"We're going to make this very easy for you," Lucas said quietly. "You can tell yourself you didn't have a choice." He glanced at Russell and then back to hold David's eye contact. "I don't want to harm you, but I will if I have to."

"Lucas." The words were choked in his throat. "Don't do this."

"You're going to tell us where Valerie is."

"What makes you think I know where she is?"

The corners of Lucas' mouth turned up slightly, but he said nothing.

"What makes you think I'd tell you if I did?"

Russell sighed deeply.

"David. You've been an asset to the Corporation. Don't play these games with us, it does you an injustice."

"An injustice? An asset?" David tasted metallic anger at the back of his throat. "The way my wife was an asset? The way Valerie was?"

"There's no need for this." His calmness was infuriating.

"No. It's a choice I'm making," David said. "I still have a choice. Lucas, *you* still have a choice." He blinked away furious tears. "Was Valerie an asset to the Corporation, as you took her blood samples, as you fed her intravenously?"

Lucas reached out and took the gun in his hand, pointing it casually at David. He raised his eyebrows, waiting for a response.

"Was Sarah an asset? The one you poisoned? How many people do you have to kill to make the Corporation work?"

Russell pushed his chair back from the table and slowly stood, rebuttoning his suit jacket. David realised then that he'd only ever seen the man in his lab coat. He seemed taller somehow, out of the underground facility.

He walked toward the door and paused to stand beside David for a moment.

"You have always been valued by the Corporation," he said without looking at him. "It's disappointing that to have to let you go."

He walked out of the room. A moment later David heard the front door of the house open and click shut again.

Lucas and David stared at each other.

"I raised you like my own," David said.

Lucas pulled the trigger. There was stillness, as the world warped and reformed into a new one without David Newlin in it. It wasn't a better world. Or a worse one. It was a world full of dangers and lies; laughter and rain. But, as the cogs of history turned, David's absence from the future was noted. And almost as soon as it happened, the world recovered its step and marched on.

Lucas put the handgun on the table, stood and walked out of the kitchen, stepping over David's body. As he reached the door he muttered over his shoulder to the security men.

"The usual disposal."

He walked out of the house into the rosy dawn and joined Russell in the electric cart on the street.

"We'll need to find her known associates," Russell said, not looking at him. "The people who hacked into our system. I want no loose ends."

"The search has already begun."

Chapter Twenty

Ava's dreams twisted and writhed behind her eyelids, tortures and narrow escapes with a cast of former friends and long-lost family members. Then she was alone, on the deck of a wrecked wooden ship, the last of a crew of pirates all gone into the depths. There was something below her, she knew, the boat was breaking up and she could feel the murmuring of an ancient threat reaching out, a skeletal hand showing just underneath the surface of the water, and then another. Hands all around her, bones and claws, hands reaching up from the depths to take her down into the deep where the blue turned black and souls were emptied of their secrets. In the dream she fought off the hands that were grabbing, pawing, latching onto her ankles and clothes. Finally, alongside one hand, a head and torso emerged from the depths. Her father who was long dead. His face was a mask of grey decomposition, lips chewed off by sea life and eyes staring and white.

"Why would you leave us?" her dad's corpse said. "Why would you leave your family?"

"I didn't Dad, you're dead!" she screamed.

"So you are you, Ava, we're all dead, we always have been." Her dad's corpse reached out and took her by the ankle in an icy grip, pulling her down into the waves.

The screams were still there when Ava woke with a start, a rush of human movement around her. It was hot. From against a wall she looked down an alleyway, bright sunshine at the end, and people moving. She squinted; her head hurt. As she found a grip on her surroundings, the memory returned, unbidden. Sophia. Her eyes saying so clearly what words could not. *Lost*. The depth of hopelessness. And then the choking. Whatever would come of the world, between Scylla and the resistance, Ava's world had ended. She lay on the concrete, willing death to open its arms. To prepare a seat for her alongside her sister, her parents, so many people she knew.

She became dimly aware when Valerie appeared by her side, but she refused to move, ignored the woman's orders and threats to go find shelter. When she next opened her eyes she saw that Valerie had brought shelter to her instead, a shade cloth was above her. She rolled over and closed herself again, closed herself to survival. She lay in a dreamless sleep that was more like death. She lay on the concrete waiting for her body to catch up with her heart.

Time passed and despite willing it to be so, Ava did not die. When she awoke, her mind was emptied and clear. Sitting up and looking around her, she realised she was in the City with no money, no sanitiser, no device. Her plastic clogs had disappeared, her feet were cut and bruised from the frantic escape. She was still wearing a stolen lab coat, which she pulled closer for comfort, feeling alien in a familiar world. Feeling unnecessary somehow.

At the end of the alley, out in the white hot sunlight, she spotted Valerie's shaved head. She was talking to someone. Bartering. As she watched Valerie turned towards her with bottles of water and bananas in her hands. She made her way into the alleyway and grinned at Ava, lifted up her trophies, like she'd prepared a meal of solid gold. Her head looked naked in the sun, her limbs strangely small inside her scrubs. The machinery of life would keep rolling whether Ava herself was part of it or not. But Valerie, like Sophia, was the fuel. As she approached, her grin took on an uncertainty, her eyes probed Ava for trauma. For some hint that things would be okay. Ava smiled.

"Can't believe you're bringing me breakfast."

"Don't get used to it."

They ate hungrily and once satisfied they walked out into the square. Around them the market had burst into life, the usual stalls doing their usual business. There was a wariness to people's expressions but also a camaraderie. They made their way through the noisy marketplace. Ava had an urge to warn Valerie about the street kids, but looking at her she could see she didn't need to. The tourist she had met a week or so ago had gone. In her place was a pale, strong, shaved-headed woman Ava barely recognised. Noticing a street kid, Valerie stopped and gave the rest of the bananas away. So like Sophia. She caught Ava's eye and grinned.

Sitting in the shade at the edge of the square, Valerie turned to her, her smile evaporated.

"You know, there's Scylla Complexes all over the world," she said. "They could be doing the same thing at every location."

"The virus?"

"Something Scylla created." Valerie shrugged. "It could be a lie altogether."

Ava watched the people, noticing a few shaved heads of research subjects standing out in the crowd. The crowd seemed to part for them as though reluctant to touch their suffering. Where would they go now? Ava wondered. How would they survive? How would anyone? The thought followed with a hollow ring in her mind. The scale of loss was too great for Ava to hold in her head. It felt swollen inside her. The coil in her spine blinked.

"How do we stop it?" Ava said, turning back to Valerie's serious eyes.

"We?"

"I'm in," Ava shrugged. "I lost my sister to this. She tried to tell me not to bury my head in the sand." Tears sprung into her eyes, surprising her into silence. She waved Valerie's concern away.

Valerie gave Ava a moment, averting her gaze.

"I have nothing else Valerie. It's fight—or stop living."

Valerie peered at Ava closely, as though trying to read her future in her eyes. She reached out and touched her shoulder tentatively.

"The world couldn't bear that, Ava," she said. "The world needs survivors."

Sitting side by side, watching the new world go by, the women didn't speak to each other for a time.

"Your dad," Ava said eventually. "We'll wait for him?"

Valerie respond with a tilt of her head.

"Yes," she said. "But not too long. He couldn't believe me about Lucas. He went back for him."

Valerie leaned into Ava, her face crumpling as the reality of her father's sacrifice, her loss of everything hit home. Ava had been living with a similar chasm, an emptiness that couldn't rest. She didn't realise that she had spent so long waiting for the bad news, knowing with certainty that Sophia was never going to return to their little room, never going to return to the bar, a quiet life of survival for the two sisters. She put an arm around Valerie's shoulder.

She watched people moving around the market—buying and selling. Living. Suddenly, she felt free, somehow, in a way she could never explain to Valerie, or to anyone else. Tears coursed down her face. Sometimes survival wasn't enough. The world had changed overnight, it was open, the walls had come down. Ava wasn't sure if it was better or worse, but at least it was honest. Sometimes when the world was ending you needed to take a stand, you needed to cast your bet and let the chips fall where they may. Ava felt reborn. She knew that her future wasn't one of just existing. And now she had someone who understood.

"I'm so sorry, Valerie."

"I am too, Ava. I am too."

Chapter Twenty-One

Russell Smart watched the pilot make the final checks and prepare for take-off with anxiety writhing in the pit of his stomach. He held the box on his lap, the vials inside wrapped in cotton wool, packaged in foam, and finally installed in a stainless steel case. The grey steel belied the aggressive lethality of its contents and Russell found himself stroking it, as if it were a nervous animal he could calm.

There would be no calming it though. The weaponised virus was as close as he could get to perfect. It was a beautiful organism, silent, secret and 100 per cent lethal. He had grown attached to it, his creation, he felt he had nurtured it into being, protected it from the ravages of politics. And now, like a parent, he was anxious about its inevitable release into the world.

The plane's engines roared as it fought and overcame the grip of gravity, launching into the air and banking, making a turn to take it into the northern hemisphere. Towards the battle lines where soldiers died over food, water, oil. It was all power, as it had been through history. Power and control and the desire to live in ever greater comfort.

Russell relaxed slightly as the plane settled into its course. There was no turning back now. He extended his legs in the empty cabin, still holding his precious cargo on his lap. He wouldn't sleep, he knew. He couldn't. Not on this flight, as the virus sat ready for its first outing. He doubted he'd ever sleep again. He sat, for hours, flying through the day and into the night, his head turned to the window. He gripped his virus, his gift to humanity, the product of his career, and stared, until his eyes were unable to penetrate the darkness gathering around him.

The sun grew low as Valerie and Ava walked toward the riverbank. The dock was heaving, boats and fishermen jostling for space around the shore. Stall holders were in front of boats haggling over seafood, salesmen were hollering their bargains into the crowd.

They stood together and looked out over the water. The river itself was vacant. The resistance fighters were mixing with the boat owners; she saw people in scrubs buying dried noodles to cook later. It was an evolution of sorts. It was survival. As long as Ava could remember the Scylla people had stayed clear of city centres, they'd eaten processed food and drank purified water. They'd had medicine. Life outside the Complex had been one of disease, death, and making ends meet, with Scylla guarding the gates to a world of plenty. Now, she could see a time where there would be no gates. The plenty was all around them, just as dangerous as ever.

There were few willing to risk the fragile equilibrium by pursuing grudges. People had gone back to work, back to the business of living. Somehow, the sense of community was more important now the world knew what monsters lurked under it all.

Short Stories

Innovative Storage Solutions

This is the second brain-space retrieval claim form Jasmine has filled out this month. The first one was lost. The form, not the brain.

As far as Jasmine knows her neural capacity is still where it has been for the past 20 years. Inside someone else, a rich person who can afford the lease. It's there filtering and processing whatever rich folks put into their minds. It's none of Jasmine's business what that might be—she signed a waiver. For 20 years she gave up all custodial rights to the grey matter. But now, the lease has expired. That rich person, whoever it was, will have to find another storage solution. She can claim hers back. She can be whole.

So here she is again, logging date of birth, date of donation, tracking numbers, claim references, all in triplicate.

Through the window, under the shade of a huge jacaranda tree, other claimants stand in a despondent cluster. The Office of Bio-Organic Storage Transfers is open for business 24 hours a day, seven days a week. There are so many people to process. Brain-space is big business. The queue could be anything from four to six to 16 hours long. Often people give up. But as time goes by, your brain needs that space back. The world is saturated in information. It drips from screens and circuits, and over time becomes a torrent. The brain-space Jasmine needed at 19 is nothing compared to the processing she needs to do at 39. She needs her neurons.

Everyone takes a number. Forms against a wall just inside the door. Orange plastic chairs line up in rows, filled with waiting claimants, all gripping a paper ticket. Some are sleeping, their heads lolling down, quiet snores emanating. Smokers take their tickets outside to chain smoke. The jacaranda is gripped by a bougainvillea vine, and is slowly being strangled.

Watching the smokers, Jasmine finds herself wondering if cigarettes damaged brain space. She has been hoping for years that hers had been leased by a teetotaller. Praying it wasn't installed inside a Crysalis user. She guesses the wealthy would have better, cleaner means to get high, but she still can't help but worry. She feels protective of her neurons, like they're her children, out there in the world. She hopes they've been taken good care of.

She grits her teeth as she fills out the Reason for Claim field, blue pen tracing an indentation on the cheap paper. She still has the original donation form, her carbon copy version, grey scribbles faded and distant after the intervening years. She was desperate back then, young, too young, and living on the street. Hugo, her partner at the time, suggested they both make a donation for the cash. But the Office of Bio-Organic Storage and Transfers wasn't interested in his brain once they found out about his drug habit. Hers though, that they eyed eagerly. She sat in a small interview room as a Transfer Ethics Assistant discussed her reasons for donating. The assistant asked about her lifestyle, her hopes for the future, with a skin deep concern for Jasmine's wellbeing playing about her lips. And then, after surgery and a truncated recovery time, Jasmine had the 10,000 credits in her account, a vial of painkillers, and a case number.

She and Hugo paid a month in advance for a damp flat, where she was visited by a community nurse occasionally as her mind healed. Hugo had a never ending list of errands to run, which in her drugged state she barely processed. She lay in bed, listening to the neighbours fighting, only the footsteps and violence trundling up and down the halls outside her door for company. The cash bought them that door, which kept the pounding steps and fists at bay. After it healed the scar was barely visible. The cash was equally insubstantial—there one minute, and after Hugo had paid his debts, and collected a supply of Crysalis, evaporated. As did Hugo in the end, when the cash ran out.

Gripping her completed form, Jasmine takes a seat on a grimy orange chair, watching the numbers tick up to those that matched her ticket. Around her sits a throng of equally glum looking claimants, each with their little paper token, their ticket to ride.

The Claims Office is nowhere near as polished as the Donations House. When Jasmine went to donate she was given free coffee and sat in crisp air-conditioning on a comfortable couch, with posters on the walls proclaiming *We Want What's Best for You* in reassuring cursive font. Now, twenty years later, she waits in an office filled with plastic chairs and filthy linoleum, a creaking ceiling fan overhead. The air is oppressive. Dense and slumber inducing. Three grey faced officials sit behind tall desks, stamping forms and directing claimants through to the next room. Each claimant approved for the next level of processing approaches the doors with trepidation. The eyes of the entire room follows them, waves of yearning crash against the grey office walls, as the doors slide open on silent rails. Everyone just wants to be whole. Jasmine needs to go through those doors so badly. She has been waiting for four hours.

She is sleepy by the time her number is called; it is called twice and the woman in the chair next to her nudges her awake. She approaches the desk bleary eyed and vague. Wordlessly sliding the claim form across, she watches the official peer at it with disappointment, as though Jasmine had delivered a stinking dog turd.

"Nearly twenty years to the day," Jasmine says with a brightness she doesn't feel. "Hopefully it will be second time lucky for me, the last form was lost."

Even as she does it she doesn't know why she is trying to start a conversation. The official, a middle-aged woman, simply lifts one eyebrow and fixes her with a long look.

"Oh, it's fine, these things happen, it's a big office after all." Jasmine's smile hurts. The official looks at her for a moment longer, and redirects her attention to the paperwork. Jasmine drops the smile and twists her fingers around each other. The waiting, the forms, they have challenged her right to the edge of her cramped brain space. Her mind throbs.

"Says here you made the donation at a suburban office," the woman monotones. Jasmine isn't sure if it's a question or not, but nods helpfully anyway.

"Suburban donation is a different claim form," the woman says. Jasmine looks at her dully.

"This form is pink," the woman continues, with great effort, as though Jasmine were a small child. "You need the green one." She waves her hand toward the racks of papers by the door.

"Fill out another one and take a number."

Stunned, Jasmine collects her paperwork and wanders over to the forms, glancing at the bougainvillea throttling the flowering tree outside. She feels a sudden kinship with the jacaranda. The air is stifling. She fills out a new form. Takes a number. She waits. The wait is eternal. The desperation thick as the air around her. Periodically a number is called out mechanically through tinny speakers. Jasmine watches as, sitting on the floor, a woman opens a hamper and starts to dish out noodles and soup from a thermos. A row of power outlets bristles with chargers for mobile phones. Outside the smokers puff away.

Six hours later, she stands in front of the same dour official, who gazes at the new, green, claim form with a dejected air.

"Twenty-year claim, then?" she intones.

"Yes." Jasmine's smiles have gone extinct. She has been at the Claims Office for twelve hours.

"I must remind you that under the Bio-Organics and Fluids Transfers Act that the Office of Bio-Organic Storage and Transfers takes no responsibility for any damage done to bio-organics during or after their lease including, but not limited to, damage, destruction, loss, theft, permanent disability or death. Do you understand?" the woman glances up at Jasmine from her computer screen.

"Er, yes?"

"Do you want to proceed with the claim?"

"Yes."

The woman strikes the papers with a stamp, rather more violently than Jasmine thinks necessary, and hands it back to her. She thrusts her head in the direction of the silver sliding doors.

"Go through," she says.

Jasmine turns to the sliding doors, eyes wide, as a hush falls over the waiting room. Every face swivels towards her, the ceiling fan groans in the sudden silence, as she approaches the gleaming interior. Somewhere, behind those doors, is the final approval, the final reinstatement of her neurons, the piece of her that has been out in the world all these years. Anxiety trills through her. She feels the longing of the people sitting in the orange chairs, she senses the desperation of the smokers outside, she catches a glimpse of the pale purple jacaranda blossoms as the tree struggles on. They all seem to will her forward and she is swept up in their desire, their wish to be whole. The doors open automatically as she steps in front of them and, after a slight pause, Jasmine swallows hard and steps through, into a quiet, warm room.

The doors close silently behind her and an official is there to greet her. Even before he speaks her hopes are quashed by the oppressive air, the stillness, the mood of long evaporated hope in the room.

"Claim form?" he says, holding out his hand.

Jasmine hands it over, her heart in her mouth. Her storage space, part of her, somewhere in the building, slumbering under deep electronic refrigeration.

The officer scrutinises the form.

"You need a Twenty-Year Claim form and a Bio-Organic Rights Waiver Form," he nods at yet another bank of forms to Jasmine's right. "That's the blue one and the red one."

Jasmine's eyes follow his gesture to the forms lining the wall, she takes in the green plastic chairs lined up in rows, filled with waiting claimants, all gripping a paper ticket. Some are sleeping, their heads lolling down, quiet snores emanating.

"Fill them both out and then take a ticket," the officer continues. Behind him a man is serving what looks like beef stew into a bowl out of an electric slow cooker. A clutch of children gather around with plates in hand. Across from him a woman with a set of knitting needles and basket of wool measures an infant with a tape measure. Jasmine is gripped with envy for the small child's wholeness.

The officer hands Jasmine's paperwork back and as she takes it he leans in to whisper conspiratorially.

"I have to warn you, you're in for a bit of a wait."

Hope Wanted

I printed it clearly on the form:

HOPE WANTED.

Toying with the pen, I stalled. Is that all? The old clock on the wall above my head ticked like a challenge. "And? And? And?" it said.

I looked at what I'd written and decided it was enough. It said all that needed saying.

The office was quiet in the mid-afternoon, but washed out clerks still scurried back and forth. Outside the heat burnt down on an empty street. Resistance posters still covered the building walls, faded, from a barely remembered moment of strength. Gone now. I waited behind a sign that said QUEUE HERE. A glum ceiling fan squeaked as it rotated. On the wall beside the counter an electronic ticker scrolled through commodity prices: Anger: 1 cent. Resentment: 3 cents. Honesty: 11 cents.

Eventually a man in a brown suit noticed me and took the sheet of paper with my carefully counted cash.

"I'm sorry Ma'am, you must have made a mistake," the clerk said, peering over his glasses. He was thin in a way that suggested some lack of a vitamin. Or not enough hugs.

I took the form from him and squinted at it.

"No, it's right. All correct."

The clerk's eyebrows creased together. He was wrestling with himself, I could tell. He wanted to ask what my story was. Along with the hot, dusty walk to between the office and whatever crumbling apartment tower he called home, this inner turmoil was probably the most activity he would have all day.

"It's just, there must be some out there," I said, by way of explanation. "Surely Hope can't evaporate."

The man's eyes wandered as he pondered it.

"Religion disappeared," he offered.

"But that's a structure," I said. I put my old handbag down on the counter, warming to the conversation now. I had been thinking about this a lot. "There's a whole apparatus around Religion that needs to be maintained. Hope isn't like that. Where could it go?"

He looked at the form again and exhaled. I smelt dust and duty on his breath.

"Do you know what I think?" I asked him. His glasses made his eyes unnaturally wide. "It's like supply and demand."

He blinked.

"Hope versus Fear, and one undermines the other," I continued. "We've got too much fear."

He nodded slightly, in acknowledgement or agreement I couldn't tell.

"There's a glut of Fear on the market, that's for sure," he said as he stamped the form.

"There's an afternoon special, so here, perhaps get a little extra protein powder for tonight." He handed back two of my coins with a watery smile. "But if you'd like, you could invest what you saved in Anger. Very cheap today."

I glanced at the coins in the palm of my hand. The electronic ticker scrolled: Jealousy: 4 cents. Sense of Achievement: 10 cents. Guilt: 6 cents.

"How much for Love?"

The man recoiled, aghast.

"Love?!" he exclaimed with a smile. "We haven't had Love in stock for, oh, donkey's years!"

He looked around at his beige colleagues as though I had told a joke, then leaned towards me, conspiratorially.

"You know, Desire is pretty good though," he said. "And not as pricey as you might think."

I smiled and shook my head.

"You know, I might save this." I put the coins in my handbag. I'd already decided I would buy some cat food on the way back to the abandoned weatherboard house I had found to hole up in. Not protein powder. Humans need something to chew. Simple pleasures. "I'll hold out for Hope."

The Wasteland

The tree was the only thing Salvador could see before the horizon. It was a relief to the eye in the desert pitted with craters and rocks. The tree leaned into the gentle incline, as though it too pushed forwards, with unsteady carbon fibre legs, into the distance. A few grim leaves clung to one of its branches, seemingly kept alive by will alone. Salvador walked directly towards it. The bodies of a human man and young boy lay, parched and shrivelled at its roots.

He paused as he looked at their emaciated shapes, weighing the need to check their remains for anything of use against his programming, which said let them rest in peace. And under it, a deep revulsion for their humanity. Their unsealed eyelids revealed pale unseeing eyes. Decomposition robbed them of definition, left only slack jaws and animal husk, food for the earth beneath them. He looked up at the handful of unlikely leaves holding on to the branches above him.

He prodded a shrunken looking canvas bag experimentally with a hinged toe. The gears in his knees whirred as he knelt to examine the prone adult figure and tapped pockets with reluctant fingers. He found a weapon and, finding it without power, dropped it by his feet. The canvas bag was filled with parchment, old and fragile. Salvador recorded the runes inscribed into it, microprocessors churning slowly. The information sat cued, along with the record of his journey, ready for upload when the satellite completed its next pass. If the satellite completed its next pass. Finally, he dropped the canvas sack, leaving the paperwork inside, at his feet by the corpses.

Salvador turned his gaze back towards the horizon. He had been walking for 600 days, east to west, as the sun had followed him in its predictable arc. His last command had been to march, to seek satellite connection. But the blinking lights had been absent overhead; the only celestial bodies had been the sun and the moon, traversing the sky with the regularity of eons. Without further contact to the network, he had no choice but to continue to search, to hope the three blinking dots at the upper right corner of his visual cortex would resolve into the connection symbol. His coordinates would be mapped, his information recorded. He would receive further orders. But for 600 days, the blinking dots had remained: connection pending.

He left the tree, continued his march west, into the horizon receding over the edge of the planet's belly. His thinking had become compromised over time, he knew. He had started to consider the vastness of space beyond the atmosphere in the abstract, not the vacuum scattered with rocks and dust he knew it to be but as a celestial playground. A waltz of cosmic proportion, within which his own expectations, a satellite, a connection, lay as a thin and paltry smear on a larger scheme.

Irrational thought, lingering within his processes, born of the whims of some ancient, long dead programmer. He enraged himself, indulging in this human-scale abstraction. There was no time to imagine, no place for philosophy. He had a command to follow, the path of the planets overhead, the sun and the moon, were of no consequence.

He charted the most direct course across the landscape ahead. He walked through the night and as the dawn filled the sky with soft reds behind him, silvery light tinting the clouds overhead, he continued, always westward. Every thirty days he stopped. Sat in a protected place and allowed his systems to reboot. Five hours out of every 730 was spent rebooting. When his system had re-calibrated, power cells replenished, he stood, his joints creaking as sand, rain and the constant marching took their toll on his gears and hinges, and continued his journey.

The landscape was irregular, vast plains rolled out for miles around him at times, then gave way to hideously deep ravines. More than once, Salvador's path through a desert or dense jungle stopped abruptly at an expanse of water, forcing him to seal his joints and sockets before stepping into the foamy waves. He walked along the ocean floor, navigating underwater chasms and peaks. Eventually the loamy ground would follow a steady incline, and he emerged on a sandy beach, breakers challenging his gyroscopic balance, ocean plant life clinging to his recessed ankle joints and toes.

On day 768, Salvador lost the use of his left arm. The gears inside whirred insistently, but some connection had been severed.

On day 801, after staggering up a sharp incline, he sat at the peak. The weight of the useless arm was an annoyance, and the repair-needed icon in his display blinked with increasing urgency that Salvador was unable to address. Disconnecting the limb at tiny bolts and screws, he abandoned it on the loose gravel. It gathered dust, blown into its crevices by the wind, as he walked away.

It was day 847 when the edifice appeared, small and distant, on the horizon. Eventually, it towered over him as he stood recording all he could of the structure for upload. It was steel and glass, a tower into the atmosphere, as tall as the mountains he had scaled, and as sheer as some of the cliffs he had been forced to avoid, backtracking around their impassive blank faces.

The monstrosity was in ruin, shattered glass lingered in steel frames, eyes blind to the world, vegetation taking the structure into its slow embrace. The tip of the spire disappeared, a glinting, spider web fine tip in the pale blue sky. Recording the entire thing required a slow circuit around it, Salvador picked his way over and around smaller squat structures at its base, dwarfed by their tall cousin.

Some part of Salvador enjoyed this work. The architecture of humanity, crumbling though it was, far outlasted the impermanent bodies and minds that birthed them. The even, parallel lines and perfect right angles pleased his processors, and he quickly mapped the structure down to the finest detail, ensuring it could be reconstructed in some distant future. Having recorded everything he could, he picked his way through abandoned domiciles and vehicles and crossed a crumbling bridge. Before long, he found himself alone in expanses of blank, natural landscape, the vestiges of life clawing back dominance on the planet's surface.

On day 1007 the hinge in his right ankle seized up. He limped onward, under a scorching sky.

It was day 1200 when he spotted a tree in the distance across a pitted plain. It leaned into the incline of the landscape, the only thing to break the unforgiving ground for as far as Salvador's ocular lenses could see. He gravitated towards it under the glaring sun. The shadows grew long as the sun sank lower over the horizon in front of him, and the tree's shadow branches clawed, desperate and yearning, across the earth. When he stood under it, he saw others had also been drawn to its paltry shade; the skeleton of an adult human and a smaller one, a child, lay under its limbs. He surveyed the decomposition, assessing the salvage opportunities. The humans' eye sockets stared blankly at him, their teeth gleamed in an eternal grin. He picked up a weapon and, finding it out of power, tossed it to one side. At his feet a canvas bag bulged slightly. Within it, reams of parchment, inscribed with unfamiliar runes. His lenses recorded their shapes, as he flicked through the pages, eventually he returned them to the bag, which he dropped into the dust by his feet.

He turned west, as the sun melted, heavy and red, into the horizon. His last command had been to walk, to seek connection with the satellite. He had been marching 1200 days watching the three blinking dots in the upper right corner of his display. Every thirty days he would stop and perform his routine reboot. He watched the three blinking dots, waiting for it to find the connection, waiting for the satellite to pass overhead. If it ever passed overhead. The only satellites he saw were the celestial bodies, performing their gravitational arc of eons.

Under the curve of the horizon, the sun bled away, its death leaving a new deep blue sky under which Salvador limped, mechanical joints creaking, always west, through the night, across a vacant planet.

At the End of the World

There was something wrong with the dog. That was how it started.

He wasn't in pain, not at first. He followed me out to the traps, snuffling along the undergrowth, nose to ground. He still curled up on the floor next to me at night, enveloping me in his dog smell and physical dreams. Four paws twitched as his mind unravelled whatever canine secrets there are to process after the day. When it was cold he moved in closer, his muscular body fitting snugly into the crook behind my knees, his even breathing lulling me deeper into an animal sleep. Our friendship was a quiet place. A tactile place of fur and skin, and the deep, dusty scents underneath.

I bent to check a trap, a soft rabbit in it, long legs lying empty against the red dirt, the skull grotesquely bulbous above its crushed throat. The dog stared. He didn't wander off marking his territory in his disinterested, workaday manner. He just stared at me, eyes fixed, unwavering. He stared as I retrieved the rabbit and I felt his animal nature, in a way that I can't describe, a way that set my hair on end and made me reach for my knife. I felt hunted.

We made our way back to the ancient shearing shed we camped in. I carried three rabbits, their limp bodies hanging from the strap of my satchel. The sunburn was already flaring on top of last night's mosquito bites. Layers of skin damage and infection and more damage. Like the abandoned land, my history was written on me in a patchwork of scars.

As a child I had stood at the top of the low hill, looking out over this flat brown land. I remember my dad driving us out in the farm ute, coated in dust and sweat, grit in our teeth, sun in our eyes. He put his hands on his hips and arched his back, the slow unravelling of a man who was older than he looked.

"You'd think we were at the end of the world," he said to the miles of open space.

Dad was long dead when the world really did start to end. I thought of him as I moved back to the bush, buried and feeding the earth. We all became something else.

I left a fear that crept through the suburbs. A lingering shadow that made people glance over their shoulders. Then the power went out across the city. The nights were punctuated with shouts and breaking glass. The dog attached itself to me as I made my way out of the city, into the country's lonely interior. At first I tried to discourage him. But he made a good travelling companion when the road was crowded and a dog made other travellers keep their distance. I never gave him a name. It didn't seem like I had a right to.

I haven't seen anyone else for months.

As I skinned and gutted the rabbits in the shade of the shed, the dog dozed, ears flicking lazily at the odd fly. I wondered if I had imagined it. He watched keenly as I prepared an evening meal, caramel eyes following the rabbit flesh into the fire and out again. We shared our food like we always did, eating in companionable silence only interrupted by the dog's enthusiastic chewing.

But later that night he began to itch. It wasn't regular dog-business, this itch, it was deep down whole body scratching. A possession, not a reflex. He scratched for hours, making me anxious, until eventually I put him on the other side of the shed, in a gated sheep pen. He sat there scratching, whimpering slightly, as his fur came out in clumps, light and fluffy at first and then wet and bloody. I swallowed around the lump in my throat as I turned my back and left him there. I slept alone, waking with a start at every stray sound in the cold night, hearing a footfall in every gust of wind.

By morning the dog lay exhausted on the bare concrete slab, foam at the corner of his mouth, his lips pulled back showing black gums and long white teeth. His thick yellow fur lay around him in clumps, laden with industrious flies. His skin was scratched raw, peeling off thick and bloody. When I bent down he issued a low, throaty growl. I backed away. He was sick. He wasn't acting himself. But the infection could only last so long, surely?

I stayed close to the shed all day, fixing broken traps, patching the makeshift mosquito net that never seemed to work. Every now and then I checked on the dog but there was no change.

He lay still, his muscles exposed and glistening. I made a few valiant attempts to keep the flies off him but it was for nothing. They swarmed.

The sun was getting low when I heard it. The shadows clawed through the bush, long and sinister, and I was certain I heard the gate to the sheep pen open. In a patch of sunlight cast on the concrete through the open door of the shed, was the dog. What was left of the dog. He swayed, as he stood on his hind legs, his new visceral coat wet in the dimming light. He lifted his head, met my eyes, his lips somehow shredded to show acres of teeth, bestial and vicious. From within the cage of his bones came a noise, a low roar, a threat. I drew my knife.

I don't know how long we stood like that. Time became elastic as I gauged the danger in those glistening teeth. I waited for the spell to break, for my friend to come back. My only friend at the end of the world. But he stared endlessly, through black eyes. He swayed, and shook dropping clods of red flesh wetly to the concrete floor. Finally, as the sun sank to its lowest ebb and the light came through the open door red and blinding, I saw. Underneath the fur and the raw, red skin, and behind the chunks of flesh that he still clawed from himself, a row of grinning ribs. White and bloody, more appeared as he shook off his mammalian skin. At the end of the world we all shed our skin. We all become something else.

I watched as he shone, black eyed and hungry. His teeth dripped and he edged forward.

In a flash, he lunged. My knife gleamed dully in my hand, his roar filled the world, and I lashed out. There was a solid thump and the dog-creature lay dead, heavy, across me, my hand gripping the knife buried in his chest. Along my right shoulder, his claws had opened four deep ravines in my skin. I breathed deep and shuddered.

I buried him behind the stump south of the shed. If you're reading this, the remains aren't human, they aren't dog, they are something else. Something unnameable. I'm writing this to tell you that you should keep walking, leave this place, keep going west. There's something here, something in the air or the water, some parasite. It got the dog, the dog nearly got me. I don't think it's safe here. I've started to itch.

Acknowledgements

"At the End of the World" was first published by *SWAMP Writing*.

"The Wasteland" was first published by *Dark Magic: Witches, Hackers and Robots*.

"Innovative Storage Solutions" and "HOPE WANTED" were first published by *Slink Chunk Press*.

SURVIVAL is a strange unlikely creature. It was dragged into the world by whimsy and curiosity and the question *what if?* Like a child that seemed destined not to make it, only to surprise everyone, it had many generous people who contributed their time and energies to nurturing and feeding the ideas that allowed it to grow. Thank you to Melissa McEwen, Kath Fleen, Michelle Nugent, Jane Rawson and the many other readers who helped shape Survival's development. Thank you to Rebecca Freeman and Amanda Rainey who shared my vision. Thank you to everyone who put up with my obsessing over cover designs. Most of all thank you to Mike, whose constant advice like "add more giant squid" is always solid, and to Kraken and Skaro who contributed literally nothing to the whole endeavour.

Finally, thank you to Jacqueline, who taught me how to read.

With gratitude to my Kickstarter backers:

Melissa McEwen

Bryce Undy

Annamarie Hepburn

Jax Razza

Michael Smith

Dave

Amanda Mitchell

Jane Rawson

Claire Nuan

Ruth Shipp

Thomas Bull

Laura Robertson

Michele Nugent

Madelon Smythe

Michelle Chomïak

Tennille D'Silva

John Hellin and Katarina Farkas

Starmen

Kimberly Sivage

Alexander Lyle

Benita Hube

and

Those who choose to not be named

Biography

Rachel Watts is a former journalist and a writer of speculative and literary fiction. She has a Master's Degree in Media and Communication and has been published in *Island*, *Westerly*, *Tincture*, *Kill Your Darlings* among others. She lives in Perth, Western Australia.

www.ingramcontent.com/pod-product-compliance
Lightning Source LLC
Chambersburg PA
CBHW071107100726
47908CB00008B/2299